MW00815420

Parlons Café
(And the Journey Through A Transcendental Love)

Lisa A. Forrest

To the individuality

of *LOVE*.

Don't let anyone define your experience of Love

for you...

~*L.A.F.*~

Table of Contents

Acknowledgements

I've been writing for most of my life, but it's been hard for me to focus enough to accomplish a book. So, for a while, I took to blogging, and that gave me the forum to write in mini story form. That turned out to be the perfect platform for me to write short, focused articles. It also helped me to express myself enough to learn to control my minds flow of information. I needed to learn patience in telling my story from beginning to end without losing focus.

So, I've been in school for the past four years to get my bachelor's degree in business administration. The last class that I had was a humanities honors class. Somehow, I managed to be the only student in my class, and I happened to have an awesome professor, Professor John Murphy. This was my second humanities class, and my first class was already one of my favorites. This class would be put in the same category, but this one would be life altering for me.

I had the opportunity to write my course project essay on a subject involving existentialism, a philosophy that I was quite interested in learning more about, since I have had a great interest in, and have read many writings of and about Friedrich Nietzsche, for many years now. I also did my last humanities course project on Nietzsche.

The research that I had to do for this project, and the information, articles, movies, and books that Professor Murphy suggested to me on the subject, was life enriching for me. My essay, and listening to the suggested audio book "At the Existentialist Café" by Sara Bakewell, inspired me greatly to start writing this book, and I haven't been able to stop until my conclusion of it.

I have finally written a novel, a feat that I have dreamed of for most of my life. And even if no one likes it, or understands it, or appreciates it, I am more ecstatic about it than anyone could know. And my humanities class and Professor Murphy, along with Ms. Bakewell's book, helped me to believe in the fact that every bit of my words are worthy of this monumental accomplishment of my own lifetime. A legacy that no one can take from me or my existence.

Transcend~

To rise above or go beyond the limits of~
To triumph over the negative or restrictive aspects
of~

To rise above or extend notably beyond ordinary
limits (Merriam-Webster).

Preface

Who gets to define a person's love for another person? Society, family, friends, the two-people involved, or the individual who feels love? Why is unrequited love seen as something that's sad and pathetic? Friedrich Nietzsche, compared the drive to knowledge, with unrequited love, "…as indispensable to us as is to the lover his unrequited love, which he would at no price relinquish for a state of indifference…" The experience of love for the individual is heart filling beyond the pain or longing that may result from it. Love can be as individual as the person feeling it, but you see it defined by many in a variety of ways, but is it truly definable in a concrete way? I say *no*, it isn't.

Love is a feeling that many confuse with other things like infatuation, sex, attraction, beauty, money, power… And love doesn't require both parties to love each other, but the one whose feeling love must make sure that they are okay with the status of that relationship. And they need to make sure that they aren't giving more *of* themselves than they are giving *to* themselves. Self-Love is a prerequisite to healthy Love.

We may subjectively believe that the person who our loved one is in love with, isn't good for them, but it's ultimately their decision. We can't tell anyone who they should or shouldn't love, and we cannot control that. A person's love for another is a personal and deep-rooted feeling, that can't be controlled by our wishes to want the best for our loved one, and we shouldn't interfere if there is no harm being done. Sometimes, as many of us know and experience, it must be a growth development. They will probably outgrow the person who we see is not in their best interest, and if they don't, maybe that's the person who they need to give them the balance that many relationships form, to get.

The Mental Orgasm

She had just finished her phone call, after telling one of her sexually explicit stories over the phone. But what she didn't expect, was the feeling that she had in the aftermath. Once she hung up, she began to feel this strange high. She felt as if she had orgasmed mentally. The feeling was like nothing she had ever felt before. It was similar to the high she felt following her physical orgasms but different. It's as if her mind slipped into a type of euphoria. She wanted to just enjoy it, but it confused her.

"Is that possible", she wondered? "Is there such a thing as a mental orgasm?" She laid back and closed her eyes, to allow herself to enjoy the feeling. Her mind was slipping into a deeply relaxed state, then started drifting into unconsciousness. She fell asleep, if only for a few minutes.

She awakened, but still felt a strange wooziness. She wanted to allow it to wear off a bit before she got up. She was still enjoying this strange euphoric feeling. Once she was able to pull herself together, she couldn't wait to text Zhon.

{Why do I feel like I'm the one who came? I wonder if there is such a thing as a mental orgasm?
Oh well, let me just enjoy it. Enjoy your day Zhon!!!}

{Lol! Thank you!!! And enjoy your day too!!!}

Charlie would only talk to Zhon about once a week or once every two weeks. He was a busy man, and her life was busy too. But when he called, she responded. His phone calls excited her greatly. Phone sex between them had become this deeply intense mental sex for her, with an intoxicating feeling after telling him her stories and audibly witnessing his release.

She noticed that when she told him stories that were actually her real experiences, that's when she felt a strange high. Telling him her made up stories still affected her, but nothing like when she told him her actual experiences. He didn't know that they were her real experiences, but one day she told him about a previous sexual encounter because he caught her off guard without a story in mind. Her reaction in the aftermath of the phone sex was strange and confusing, yet it gave her a type of high. She didn't understand it, but it felt wonderful.

She enjoyed the sporadic phone calls that caught her off guard. She would sometimes need him to lead her into a story by asking her questions, and she would respond by "pulling up" or "recalling" a story. A sort of foreplay for phone sex. This was the definition of living in the moment, for her. These phone calls would always leave her high.

One time she wondered what she'd do if he'd call her while she was driving. She realized that she wouldn't be able to drive and tell him a story too. The state of mind that she would be in, wouldn't allow her to concentrate on the road at the same time.

She also realized that it was hard for her to create stories during these phone calls. In the beginning, when she would tell him made up stories, they were stories that she had already come up with, so she didn't have to create one as she told it. But when she tried to do it *during* their phone calls, she couldn't; and that's what led her into telling true stories. This fascinated her because it told her that whatever part of her brain affected her sex drive, wouldn't allow her to use the creative part of her brain at the same time.

Sex was always an extremely pleasant experience for Charlie. The end result of an encounter was a relaxing, stress relieving, pleasurable, occurrence. No wonder she enjoyed sex so much. Nothing else in life felt that way to her. And she didn't need to be in love or have a deep emotional connection to enjoy this feeling. She just had to have a connection and deep attraction to her partner.

But the experience with Zhon went a bit further. The feeling was beyond pleasurable. The psychological connection of verbally bringing him into her deeply intimate encounters with other men was a sort of deep catharsis. She was sharing her most intimate encounters and trusting him with them. When she finally told him what she was doing, she took a chance of him rejecting her, but he never did.

She always knew that it was never a good idea to tell any man about other men. She had learned that most men couldn't handle that much truth about a woman's sexual past, even though he knew she had one. Knowing that she had one was one thing, hearing the intimate details of it was another. Having a mental picture of the woman you're dealing with sexually, with other men, isn't something that most men would handle well unless she was someone who they just used for sex. And Charlie didn't rule that out with Zhon, but she didn't feel that way about him.

They were friends outside of the sex, and he had become her confidant to whom she told some of her deepest thoughts to, along with venting to him and even confessing things to him. He always accepted these things with interest and care. She never felt judged by him, and she always felt like he understood her. Every encounter between him and her, sexual or otherwise, was pulling him into a special place in Charlie's life.

The Initial Encounter

Charlie.

Charlie was a very attractive, curvaceous, light-skinned Black woman. She dressed conservatively, yet she wore clothes that accentuated her curves. She liked wearing heels, which gave her 5'5" frame more height, with her D cup bosoms, her small waist, thick hips, ample booty, and thick thighs. She wore little makeup; some lipstick, eyeliner, and mascara; but she was a natural beauty. She had brown eyes, with a round nose, and not so thick lips. She looked a bit Latin and many people had mistaken her for Hispanic, but she was proudly Black. She always had pride in the strength of her culture, descendants of American slaves. She was a 40 something divorcee with no children. She was unable to have them, but she also didn't desire them.

She kept a short haircut, because of the power that it gave her. She had long hair in her youth, but never liked it on her, so she had it cut short at a young age. She didn't recognize the strength that she derived from her close cut until she was older, but she did realize that she felt more confident with it. Maybe it was the many compliments that she received from men and women alike because it fit her well. Or maybe her artistic nature recognized what style fit her look and personality. But the true test of the power in her cut, was when she had it cut extremely close like a guys cut.

One day, she was just feeling bold, and a bit angry inside, and decided to have her hair cut really short; and dared anyone to say anything negative to her... she was ready for it. She was ready for a (verbal) fight, but what occurred instead was that she was complimented by everyone, from the barbers to the patrons in the barbershop, and people on the street. She even noticed a few stares without a word, but their expressions were of a pleasant nature, and a silent confirmation of it "fitting" her look.

That day, she would bleach her hair blonde, as a type of defiant gesture to society and everyone, but instead of ignorant stares and mean remarks like she expected, she continued to receive compliments and smiles. Her gesture of defiance backfired but in a good way. She was mentally arming herself for a fight, which developed from some internal turmoil that she was going through. But what happened instead, is that it empowered her with the confidence that she needed at that point in her life, and that feeling never left her. Every time she got a fresh haircut, she would feel an internal power that could never be taken from her. And as she maintained her short cut, she maintained her powerful feeling.

At this point, she had shaved sides with straight black hair on top, for a modified mohawk. She changed her hairstyles and hair colors, often. Each new style and color was a fashion statement and gave her the feeling similar to wearing a new outfit that complimented her curves and accentuated her femininity. She wasn't a prissy female, but a woman of strength whose sexuality was undeniable. Someone once told her that even if she were bald, no one could mistake her for anything but a woman.

Charlie was the owner of a little café that sold coffee, tea, wine, and beer, on the outskirts of Philly. They also sold hors d'oeuvre's, and pastries. She always liked a more intimate atmosphere like a coffee shop or café. No large crowds, televisions or loud music, but she did have soft music playing. Nothing to interfere with talking. She had art for sale on her walls from local artists and people she knew who were talented artists.

She opened her shop as a place for people to come to and have real live conversations again. Her five years on social media had proven to be enough for her, and she just wanted to meet real live people, and have face to face conversations; especially about things that interested her.

She had a hard time meeting people with common interests in Friedrich Nietzsche, whose words she understood and felt a connection to his philosophies. The Marquis De Sade, someone who she sometimes understood, agreed with some of his philosophies but was grateful for having a justice system to keep deranged men like him in prison. Shakespeare, for she loved many of his plays, including Othello, Hamlet, The Merchant of Venice, and Romeo and Juliet. She enjoyed discussing philosophy and psychology. It was easier to find people to talk about many of her social interests, but not always.

She also wanted a place where cell phones were discouraged, but not forbidden. The anti-social behaviors that cell phones were causing, concerned her. And she wanted to neutralize those behaviors in her café. After all, it was called "Parlons", meaning "Let's Talk" in French, which subtitled the café's name.

She owned the two buildings that were adjacent to her café on each side. To the left of the café, was her boutique that was run by her niece. She had created a fashion brand along with her niece that was geared toward savvy women who preferred and understood quality. It was a unique brand that connected with women on many levels.

To the right was her consignment shop run by another niece. She wanted to create a space for stay at home moms to have a place to sell their creations, from jewelry to clothing, to paintings… anything that anyone created themselves that was sellable. This way, they could always make money while at home tending to their children, without worrying about trying to get out to sell their creations themselves. They would have a side hustle without the need to hustle. The consignment shop would do that for them.

It wasn't just for women's art either. Many men had their artistic creations in there too. She knew that not all people had the art of the hustle in them, although they were great artists. This gave them all a place to show their talents, without the worries of selling their creations themselves.

Zhon.

Zhon was a 6'5" 40 something (although a couple of years younger than Charlie) brown-skinned man, who was of average build with long beautiful locs, wore glasses, was of high intelligence and was a journalist living in Paris, France. He was also from Philly, like Charlie, and that's where they met and began their friendship before Zhon moved to France for his work. He was freelanced, but the company who gave him most of his assignments needed him in Paris. He was also a writer who had a couple of published books, something Charlie aspired to.

Zhon was someone who was well respected for his ability to tackle social issues that weren't very popular with the "powers that be" in the U.S. and around the world. He was dedicated to his work and fighting for the rights of the Black community and for their progression through self-help and self-accountability; he believed strongly in his people.

The Encounter.

Charlie and Zhon met at a social event that was also a celebration of a mutual friend's birthday. Charlie noticed him, and he noticed her, so she took it upon herself to introduce herself. She was aware of Zhon because she followed his work and was a bit of a fan.

"Hello, Mr. Jackson! My name is Charlise Langston, but you can call me Charlie! It's a pleasure to meet you!" as Charlie held out her hand to shake his.

"Well, hello Ms. Langston, the pleasure is mine!"

He grabbed her extended hand to shake it firmly, yet gently. Charlie allowed him to lead the handshake because she could be very aggressive when she led it. His height was very noticeable to her and caused an unexpected attraction because of it. She didn't really understand why this affected her, but she liked the warm feeling she got from staring up at this towering figure of a man.

Charlie and Zhon talked about how they knew the birthday party recipient, who was a local political figure, and how they each met him. They both got a kick out of each other's stories. After their conversation, they parted ways and mingled within the crowd with other people. By the end of the party, Charlie was ready to leave a few minutes before everyone else. Zhon noticed that she looked to be leaving, so he made it over to her to give her his business card. Charlie returned the effort with giving him her business card. They both extended courtesies, then she left to go home.

Charlie received a text from Zhon that night.

{I really enjoyed talking to you! Maybe we can have lunch sometime soon?}
{What a great idea! It would be nice to sit and talk with you. Also, I would love it if you can stop by my café sometime!}
{Will do! See you soon!}

So, Zhon stopped by the café to see Charlie, two days later. She was surprised to see him. There was some very strong chemistry happening between them. You could almost cut it with a knife. Charlie greeted her invited guest…

"Hello, Mr. Jackson! What a nice surprise! How are you feeling on this beautiful afternoon?"

"I'm great! How are you feeling?"

"Wonderful, now that I have such a handsome guest!"

Zhon laughed at her complimentary comment.

"Well, well! It's nice to be appreciated!"

Charlie gave him a devilish smile. As he took his seat, she asked him what she could get for him. He just wanted some coffee and asked her what kind of cakes she had. She gave him his choices, and he chose a slice of red velvet cake with cream cheese frosting. She gave his order to Devon, her assistant, and told her to bring her the same; she then sat down with Zhon.

"I'm happy that you took me up on my offer to stop by."

"Yeah, well, I couldn't get you off my mind."

"I've actually been going through the same about you."

"Oh, Really!?!?" He said in a surprising, but almost skeptical way.

"Yes! I was saying to myself 'Damn, I would love to get him into bed!'" She started laughing.

"Wow! I said the same thing about you!"

Their eye to eye contact became deep and intense as they tried to gauge each other for honesty in their words. How could they really be thinking the same things about each other; yet they were. They stared at each other almost until discomfort, but Charlie broke the silence.

"So, what should we do about it?"

"Why don't we start by you telling me what you like."

Charlie had no problem with that, and she loved his upfront blunt approach. That alone was a turn on to her.

"I like aggressive sex, I'm very uninhibited, I'll try almost anything at least once, but no animals and no threesomes."

Zhon laughed a little, "You don't have to worry about the animals, I'm with you on that; but no threesomes, huh?"

"Nope!"

"Have you ever tried a threesome?"

"No, I have not, nor do I have a desire to."

"I can dig it! No threesomes. So, tell me what else you like."

"How 'bout you tell me some of the things that you like," said Charlie.

"Okay, well, I like to talk a lot of shit when having sex."

His profanity threw Charlie off a bit because he just didn't seem the type to use it, but it excited her coming from him.

"I like to talk dirty, I like a little ass smacking… that would be giving, not getting; and let me tell you, you have a nice ass."

Charlie's eyes got wide with surprise and excitement. And Zhon could tell she liked his revelations.

"I just want to fuck the shit out of your sexy ass, and I can't wait until that happens!"

Charlie was almost speechless, but not quite.

"Whoa!!! I didn't even think that you cussed, and what a surprise, but not in a bad way, because I like what you like. I like talking shit, and I just love dirty talk, it really turns me on, and I love having my ass smacked."

They were both sexually aroused and knew that they needed to change the subject. Devon was coming with the coffee and cake, just in the nick of time. They changed the subject and talked about how delicious the coffee and cake were. They both got quiet for a bit as they enjoyed themselves, eating and drinking. They then resumed their conversation.

"So, when do you think we can get together so that I can enjoy what you enjoy?" Zhon smiled as he stared at Charlie for her answer.

"As soon as you tell me what's good for you; my availability is open."

"How about tonight, at my place?"

"All I need is an address."

Zhon texted his address to Charlie's phone and told her to meet him there that night around 8:00 pm. She told him that she'd be there. They made a little small talk about other things as they finished their coffee and cake. When Zhon was ready to leave, Charlie walked him outside, gave him a hug, then let him know that she would see him that night. He kissed her on the cheek and said, "See you later!"

They were both as excited as teenagers waiting for 8 pm. Charlie needed to go home to jump in the shower and put on some of her prettiest underwear to wear under her outfit that she planned on wearing. She also brought a bottle of wine home to take over to Zhon's place; she chose a Prosecco.

When she got there, there were no "polite preliminaries of pretentiousness" about what was about to go down, and she really liked that about Zhon. They knew what they were both there for and didn't see the need to have unnecessary niceties. He led the way to his bedroom, and she followed. He went back downstairs to get himself and Charlie each a bottle of water. He also brought up a bucket of ice and a glass for Charlie's wine.

Charlie took a few deep swigs of her sipping wine, but there was no time for sipping. Zhon was taking off his clothes, so Charlie started taking off hers. When she got down to her underwear, Zhon walked over to her, then grabbed her and kissed her, as he removed her bra. He left her almost woozy with his kissing skills.

He turned her around with her back toward him so that he could grip her breasts and twist her nipples. She winced from the pain which released endorphins that mixed with the pleasure sensors of her nipples. This got her really worked up and ready for whatever he wanted to do to her. He remained behind her and guided her over to the bed. He told her to bend over the side of the bed and stay there. He went to get her heels so that she could put them on and give her better height for him to enter her from behind more easily.

Once she put her heels on, she bent over the bed again. Zhon pulled her panties down to mid-thigh. His erection was rock hard, and he could hardly wait to penetrate Charlie. He grabbed his penis and entered her slowly. She jumped a little as he began to enter her. He began to pump her slowly as his eyes rolled to the back of his head.

"Got Damn this pussy is good!"

Her warm soft wetness felt wonderful to him. It felt so good that he didn't want to stop, but he was almost about to climax, so he pulled out. He told her to lay on the bed, on her back. He removed her panties but left her shoes on. He told her to hold her legs open at the knees, and to pull them close to her. He entered her again, as his upper body remained elevated on his elbows. He began to pump her slowly,

"Fuck my pussy harder, baby, and faster. I need you to fuck me faster."

Zhon gave her what she wanted, and she started to breathe heavily, then began shouting from the pleasure of the intercourse. She shouted…

"Yes, baby! Give me that big fucking dick! Fuck me harder baby!"

And he did, so she couldn't talk anymore at that moment because she was shouting in ecstasy. He pulled out of her and made her get on her knees on the bed. He then penetrated her aggressively from the back, as she shouted from his deep, hard, fast, non-stop pumps. "Did you come yet b….?" He almost slipped and called her a name, but she wanted him to finish saying the word.

"Go ahead, baby! Say it! I want you to say it!"

"Did you come yet bitch? Huh? Did you come yet you fuckin' bitch?"

She had already come, but those words got her all worked up again, and as he kept pumping, she came again really hard. Zhon could feel her vagina contracting, so his words, her reactions, and the feeling of her vagina contracting around his penis, caused him to climax wildly as his body jerked from the ecstasy of it all. Charlie dropped forward into a laying position, and he dropped with her. He laid on her motionless for a couple minutes, then he rolled off and laid there with his eyes closed and his arm over his face. He needed a little time to enjoy the feeling and regain his composure; Charlie needed the same.

Charlie really liked Zhon and never expected him to be so "primal" during sex. Nor did she really understand at that moment *why* she was so extra turned on by his aggression and his profanity, but there was something different with him.

Zhon got up to use the bathroom, then when he came back, he was about to put on his boxers, but Charlie asked him not to. She said that she didn't want to be the only one nude, but what she really wanted was the skin to skin contact that she didn't get often enough, and she enjoyed the energy charge that she experienced from it.

They laid side by side in the bed, with Charlie laying in the crook of his arm, her head on his shoulder, and her right leg touching his left leg. They talked and learned some little things and some major things about each other. Then Zhon started to get a little frisky and wanted to go another round. Charlie was all about it. They enjoyed another aggressive and profane round of sex that night. A night that left them both with thoughts of moments that would last for the next couple of weeks; especially for Charlie. She could not stop thinking about Zhon or their night of pleasure.

Zhon was someone who Charlie greatly admired. She read many of his news articles and even his books. She didn't agree with everything that he wrote, but she did agree with most of it. She at least understood those things that she didn't agree with. He was someone who she respected for his integrity, his discipline, his honesty, and his fight for what's right. She saw him as someone with high moral standards, so his profanity threw her a bit. Not that a person couldn't have high moral standards and use profanity, she just didn't see him as someone who would use it; at least not in the context that he did.

None of this was a bad thing, because now Charlie saw him as more human, than someone whose morality she could never, nor would she ever, live up to; she really liked knowing that about him. He didn't allow his public personality to interfere with his private personality, and he had the ability to keep them separate. She believed in discretion as a necessary social action, to protect a person's reputation, from social judgment by people who had no right to judge you. Especially for what you do in private; although she had her moments when she didn't care who judged her for what she said or did.

As she got older, she no longer felt the need for the same discretions that were necessary as a younger woman. She also didn't feel the need for the same self-control as was necessary when she was younger. Experience and adversity forced her into living her life in the moment, by doing whatever she felt would bring her the most pleasure during that moment, and this worked for her.

Life was very much a pleasure to her, and she continued to work hard to maintain the independence that allowed her the freedom to do as she pleased. The adversities of her younger years and her ability to overcome those adversities helped her to become one of the strongest people that she knew. Those same adversities forced her to see her life as a gift and to learn to enjoy it to the fullest. For her, that didn't mean parties and living recklessly, it meant to live in a way that brought *her* the most joy. It also didn't mean to live without thought and respect for others, it meant to weigh the consequences of her actions, and to make her decisions based on what she was willing to accept and live with, should she have to pay for any decision that was made against societies rules and laws; and that's how she lived.

The Cyber Affair

Charlie and Zhon saw each other one more time before he revealed that he had to leave and move to France for his work. Charlie was a bit disappointed but wished him well; although this wouldn't end their sexual relationship, it just changed the dynamics of it.

Charlie was missing Zhon when she came up with a fantasy that she wrote into a story. She decided to send it to Zhon's email, not sure if this would be favorably accepted by him, so she followed the story with,

"There's more, but I need to make sure that this is okay to you, for me to do."

His response was, "Wow! It most certainly is okay! Please! Continue!"

His response made her smile, so she sent him another story of a fantasy scenario,

"You and I are on a Caribbean island in a villa. We are laying on the bed nude, with my head laying on your shoulder, my leg wrapped around yours, and my pussy kissing your muscular thigh. The windows are open with a warm breeze blowing through the villa. The breeze makes us both a little horny, so I climb on top of you and begin to kiss you, deeply and passionately. Your dick begins to grow right beneath my pussy and pulsates as if it has a mind of its own, and is trying to find its way inside of me. I put my hand down between us to grab your dick and help it to find its way. I slowly ease myself onto it and begin to ride it, as I lean forward and grab and twist your nipples.

You then grab my hips and help me to ride you faster, as I moan loudly from the deepness of your dick inside of me. I ride you for as long as I can, but your constant pounding on my cervix becomes overwhelming after a few minutes, so I fall off you. As I'm laying on my stomach, you enter me from the back, with your legs on each side of me. You begin to fuck me in this position hard and fast as I toot my ass up so that you can get deeper inside of me. You then put your legs between mine, to get even deeper inside of me, then I scream from the delicious pain of your deep, hard, fast thrusts. And you continue to pound me until you feel my orgasm, as my pussy contracts around your dick, and you explode from the pulsations of my climax."

Charlie ends the scenario there, and Zhon responds with, "Sheesh!!!"

She then took a break, at least for that day. She didn't want to overwhelm him with stories. She would send him sexually explicit scenario's every once in a while, to catch him off guard, and to excite him as a way for her to maintain a sexual connection to him, during his physical absence.

Charlie understood the phenomena of boredom, so she welcomed Zhon's suggestion of telling her stories over a phone call. She knew that although she sent him different types of stories, the act of her sending and him reading stories as a sexual connection would run its course, eventually. Even though it hadn't yet, it was a good time to transition to another type of cyber-sex. She would still continue to send him her stories, but less frequently. This would prevent the sent stories from losing their power because she would have another delivery system, and this would prevent this mode of cyber-sex to find its demise as a way to reach Zhon's loins.

At this point, Charlie had never really experienced phone sex, nor did she have a comfort with wanting to do it. Zhon helped to calm her anxiety about it, and let her know that all she had to do was tell the same stories verbally. Charlie's greatest discomfort about it was being able to tell her stories verbally in a way that would come across as sexy to him. Zhon had no question that whatever way she told it, it would sound sexy to him, and he would get the satisfaction that he sought.

Charlie nervously began to tell the last story that she wrote to him, from memory. With all the profane language and explicit sex that her stories entailed. This is what Zhon needed, a more involved connection of the senses. Her voice gave him a more palpable involvement of her stories. He would close his eyes and visualize what she was relaying to him over the phone. And the sound of her voice helped to make the stories more intense and pleasurable. This would become another sporadic mode of a sexual connection for them.

Charlie would also send him sexy texts as a way to stay sexually connected to him and to catch him off guard. She loved knowing that he would be in inopportune places when she sent her nasty texts and that he would become aroused by them. But she would also become a bit concerned and wanted to make sure that she wasn't causing him any embarrassment, so if she wanted to send him something really nasty, she would send it to his email and warn him that perhaps he should wait to read it in private.

They would talk once in a while about non-sex related topics. She would often send emails to him to vent, or about issues of concern so that she could get his feedback, or so that he could be a sounding board for her to evaluate her own thoughts on an issue. He became an invaluable confidant to her. Something that she never had before, and something that she found to be life-altering for her. She now understood the value in psychiatry and religious confession.

Being able to talk about your deepest thoughts and concerns, without judgment (and Zhon never judged her, or at least he never made her feel judged), to someone who was highly respected, and greatly trusted, was invaluable to emotional release and growth. It also helped her to learn about herself by way of speaking the truth out loud (whether audibly or written), realizing it comprehensively, then evaluating it as a way of learning and growing. This is one of the many invaluable things that Zhon gave her. This created a deeper trust in Zhon and a greater respect for his ability to be understanding. This meant more to her coming from him because she knew that he had a pretty high moral standard. A standard in which her actions tested over and over again, at least in her mind.

But Zhon never made her feel bad, or judged, or even pushed away from her during her most socially rejected actions. She sometimes wondered if she would tell him these things to try to push him away, in a subconscious attempt to make sure that she didn't fall for him. But he never budged, and always remained a devoted confidant to her.

Charlie knew that friendship was the apex of their relationship. They came from different worlds, in many ways, and his wants for a relationship were different from hers in an almost opposite way. Charlie had no desires to ever marry again, but Zhon made it clear that marriage for him was important and a focus of his. This understanding kept Charlie's realist perceptions in a realistic frame of thought, whenever it came to Zhon and herself.

Also, she would confide many deep, dark, feelings and actions to Zhon. Prior to her friendship with him, she understood that there were some things that you never tell a man that you have feelings for, but that limit was overridden many times with him. He knew things that most men couldn't handle about a woman who they were interested in. Things that once revealed, could end a relationship. She knew this before she chose to tell him these things, but revealing them to him as her trusted confidant, was more important than keeping them from him because of his possible judgments as a man.

So, Charlie was clear about their relationship, and she was grateful for it. He gave her so many things that she never had in any type of friendship, and sex with him took her to a place that she had no idea existed. Zhon knew that Charlie cared for him in a deep way, but he never understood exactly why. She knew that it confused him, but she would reveal her why, when she was ready.

I Wish You the Best.

Charlie sent Zhon a sexy text, but his response didn't really acknowledge the content. She wasn't sure if he was finally tired of her, or if it was something else. She then realized that maybe he was seeing someone, so, because she knew that he wasn't the type to betray a partner, she just fell back on the attempts at cybersex.

Charlie would never question Zhon about his personal life or business. He was a pretty private person, and she grew up in a household and culture where you didn't ask people personal questions because it was none of your business. This always stayed with her, and since Zhon was not her man, she would never question him about personal things. This also kept things simple between them, and she felt, if he wanted her to know something, that he would tell her; and if he didn't, he didn't, no matter what his reasons were.

Any relationship that Zhon would enter into since he and Charlie became friends, would not interfere with their friendship, but it would put their sexual connection on pause. Charlie wanted the best for Zhon and knew that the day would come when he would meet someone that he would fall in love with. Whenever she was aware of a love interest of his, she fell back and wished him well. In her mind, she always had to assume that this might be the one, so she would attempt to disconnect.

She realized early on that she had an emotional connection to him, but she was able to keep that separate from the sex. She had learned to compartmentalize sex from emotion when she still needed to satisfy her sexual needs with the husband that she no longer loved. She used this power to continue to satisfy her sexual desires, without a need to be in any relationships.

After her divorce, she eventually fell in love with a guy who loved her dearly, she could do no wrong that he wouldn't forgive. But they both had some deep issues that would prevent them from maintaining a healthy relationship. This and the failure of her marriage caused her to shut down emotionally. She no longer could see herself giving her heart to any more men. To her, love was a precious emotion and she felt that if she kept allowing men into her heart, without any long-term connection, each one would gnaw away at the preciousness of that emotion until love wouldn't be that special thing that she still felt it to be.

So, Charlie would turn away from allowing men into her heart. She would use her ability to compartmentalize sex from emotion, to allow her to maintain a sex life, without diminishing the specialness of love. Her focus became her journey to independence, which included entrepreneurship and helping others to succeed. She would also be an advocate for women's issues, and for the Black community, in her own personal way; this became her purpose.

She lived like this for many years, at least a decade. She met a couple of men along the way who she attempted a deeper relationship with, but each man had personality flaws that she had no patience for, mainly dishonesty. This just fortified her need to remain single and to do what was necessary to maintain her independence.

Charlie came from a two-parent home and was a daddy's girl and a momma's girl, so she didn't have any deep-rooted man issues that sometimes occur when there is no man in the home growing up, or if there is a bad relationship between father and daughter. She didn't *need* a man to love her because she had the unconditional love of her parents and family. Did she hope to one-day love again? She did, but she needed it to happen naturally. She didn't believe in the idea of giving ultimatums or manipulating men into being with her, especially by using sex as a tool or weapon.

She couldn't stand manipulative people and could "see them coming a mile away". Although Charlie knew her powers and knew *how* to manipulate, she would never use those powers to do harm, for any negativity, or to get or keep a man. This wasn't her style, and she had no desire to push a man to want to be with her. She also knew that this type of action, many times, would backfire. The only person that Charlie was interested in controlling was herself.

Zhon would never mention his new relationship to Charlie, but it was confirmed by a mutual friend in passing. She never asked about it, it just came up in conversation that Zhon had a new lady. Her intuitions were correct, and she silently wished him well.

I Miss Our Cyber Affair.

Months had passed since Charlie and Zhon had any cyber-sex. She wasn't sure if he was still involved with anyone, so she decided to "test the waters" by telling him that she missed their cyber-affair. He responded with "I'll call you tonight!" She didn't know what to expect, but she was excited and got the feeling that maybe he was no longer seeing anyone seriously.

So, Zhon did call her that night, and they got into their sexy conversation, and things were back to the way they used to be. She realized how much she really missed their phone calls, and the resulting feeling in the aftermath. Her mental orgasms returned, and she hadn't recognized how much she really missed Zhon, the cyber-sex, and the mental orgasms until they reignited their sex play. After the phone call, she laid back and enjoyed her high.

Charlie and Zhon would continue their cyber-sex for the next year. She would get to see him once in that year when he was in town. They would text each other sporadically, about two to four times within any month. Charlie would think about Zhon every day but didn't want to be bothersome by texting too often, and she based that on her own dislike of daily calls or texts, from anyone. She would rarely ever call, because she didn't know what times would be good for him, and she understood that he was busy and didn't always keep a routine schedule. She would sometimes be compelled to text him with little things like,

{Just thinking about you and wanted to say hey!}

or send him a wink emoji or a kiss emoji. She would from time to time need to vent to him, or "spill" her thoughts to him, just to get them out of her head. These would many times be sent to his email because they would be too long for a text message, although some would end up in a text. Every once in a while, she would feel the need to express her gratitude to him, for being a shoulder to lean on, or a sounding board to vent; and she would do this in a text, or email, depending on how much she needed to say. Charlie preferred this mode of communication because she could take the time to say everything that she wanted, with no interruptions, and with enough time to recall words that might escape her in a verbal conversation.

Many of these emails and Zhon's responses to them would touch her in a way that would cause her to reread them, over and over, until she would get her fill of them. Doing this would bring her a type of mental pleasure that satisfied her greatly. To dwell on his words and her words in print, had become a way for her to relive the feelings of the pleasure that it gave her, and it was a special type of satisfaction for her that she learned helped her with her feelings for Zhon.

When she thought about this objectively, she realized that it seemed a bit weird, but she had come to understand that how society viewed things, and how she viewed things were many times greatly different. And she refused to allow societies views to make her feel weird or crazy because she knew that she wasn't. What she understood is that her needs in life were different than what society considered as a normal way to do and view things, and she had come to terms with that many years before. She had a "fuck society and their judgments" attitude for many years, and it was important for her, to recognize what things worked for her to bring her happiness, not based on societies views of how that should look.

She greatly disliked the word "normal", because that word was different for each individual. Normal, in the eyes of society, was whatever was deemed as a religious or Christian normal, something that she did not like, because of its usual judgmental views against anything considered non-Christian, based on the policy-makers interpretation of what Christian should be. And if her normal was to be viewed as anything, many of her ways and views would be considered abnormal, based on societies standards.

Charlie believed that society spent too much time judging people and putting labels on things that they consider unconventional. This, in turn, forces many good people to believe that there is something wrong with them because they don't fall into societies idea of normal. This is such a sad state of events because this causes people to attempt to find a fix for something, that is a part of who they inherently are, just to "fit in."

A person's sexual desires are one of those things that takes a hit with this socialization. Sex has been so demonized in society, through history and religion, that people's inherent drives toward unusual desires, force them to repress themselves sexually. Repression of a feeling or desire, especially if it's inherent, many times forces itself to come out in a way that is usually ugly, shameful or harmful. But society never wants to take responsibility for creating this phenomenon. They blame the person and call him/her a deviant, pervert or even a monster as they (the judgmental) are dealing with their own shame, many times.

Charlie wouldn't become a victim of this attempt at normalization because she knew better. And she would also be a cheerleader for anyone who expressed themselves, without allowing society to force them into a box of social normalization.

During this time, Charlie would meet a guy who she liked a lot but wasn't sure how they would get along.

She wanted to give it a shot, but she let him know that she wasn't looking for a relationship at that time, although they could hang out. They would get into some verbal sex play that had her desiring a sexual connection with him. Joey was a 6'4" tall dark-skinned man, who was slim and athletically built. He had a bald head and sexy goatee.

Charlie was extremely attracted to him. He always looked nice in his ball wear and smelled divine to the point that Charlie just wanted to bite him on his neck. His attraction to her was unquestionable. They would go out a couple of times to eat and to the movies. Charlie couldn't wait to bed him, but she could tell that he was someone who might get too attached, so she wanted to make it clear what her intentions were. Those intentions were that she wasn't looking for a relationship, and she had other friends.

Joey claimed to understand, so one night they went to his place to chill. He cooked for Charlie and made her some strawberry daiquiris for her to relax. They would watch a movie together, but before it was over, they were both feeling the alcohol and getting a bit frisky. Joey began to kiss on Charlie's neck and ears. He also started kissing the back of her neck where she was extremely sensitive. He hit all the spots that other lovers missed and put her into high arousal. This guy knew what he was doing.

Joey had a tongue ring, so when he kissed Charlie with a deep, sensual, long kiss, he left her breathless. The tongue ring added an element of eroticism that she never expected. He unbuttoned her blouse, then took it off her. He then kissed her again, as he unbuttoned and removed her bra like a pro. He kissed her neck before he moved down to her breasts. He would grab them both, then gently squeezed them together with his big hands. He would then softly suck on one nipple, then the next.

His soft lips and tongue, along with his gentle sucks and licks, with the added sensation of the tongue ring, drove her absolutely wild with desire.

"Fuck me! I need you to fuck me!" Charlie said in an almost breathless plea to help end her horny discomfort. Joey got up to remove his clothes, and Charlie did the same as quickly as she could. Joey went back to his bedroom and returned with a blanket and pillow. He put them down on the hardwood floors for Charlie to lay on. She understood and assumed a position on the blanket without getting a word of direction.

Joey laid on top of her and kissed her again passionately. Charlie was already about to burst, and this put her over the top.

"Joe, I need that dick inside of me *now!*"

Joey was intentionally driving her crazy and wouldn't penetrate her just yet. Her firm, protruding nipples called him to suck on them, for his own pleasure. He would grab one breast to suck on, as he rubbed and twisted the other nipple; he was driving Charlie wild. He then kissed down to her belly, then he kissed her on each side of her groin area. He already knew that her clitoris was swollen with desire before he attended to it. It was engorged from the excitement of his expert foreplay. He spread her lips, as he put his mouth over her clit, and placed his tongue to allow his tongue ring to perfectly connect with her clitoris. His gentle and perfect sucks and licks caused her to explode in less than a minute after he connected with it.

Joey also knew that a clitoral orgasm was separate from a vaginal orgasm, so he finally penetrated Charlie to give her the well-rounded satisfaction that he knew she needed. He knew what his talents were doing to her, and he knew how to fully satisfy her. Joey's erection was super hard as he penetrated Charlie. And he knew from their conversations that Charlie liked aggressive sex, so he grabbed her legs, pressed them to her shoulders to get his erection deep inside of her, then he pounded her incessantly until she screamed herself out. Charlie had passed out from the almost unbearable back to back multiple orgasms, clitorally and vaginally. Joey's climax was pretty spectacular too. He laid on the side of Charlie, satisfied for the moment, and seemingly use to having women respond to him in this way.

The Distraction.
Charlie had heard in passing that Zhon was involved again. This would spark a deeper interest in Joey so that she could push her feelings for Zhon into relegation. Joey would call Charlie daily, and although she wasn't used to daily phone calls from anyone, she wanted to learn to be okay with it. She didn't particularly like talking on the phone, she preferred texting, or talking face to face.

Zhon called Charlie about a month after she found out that he had a new lady. He was just checking on her, and she would ask how he was doing. They had some light flirtations, but Charlie didn't want it to go too far if he was still involved.

"Aren't you involved again?"

"Yeah, something like that!"

"Well, I don't want to be your albatross... I like you too much."

They both laughed, but Charlie really didn't want to be that person responsible for any moral dilemma that may happen, with Zhon in particular, when couples have fights or arguments that motivate some to cheat on their mates. And even though she and Zhon were thousands of miles away, she still didn't want to pull him into any phone sex knowing that he was involved with someone.

She didn't want to be that person, with him. His moral standards and integrity were two of the many things that she admired in him, so she wasn't going to be the one to compromise any of those admired qualities.

Zhon's friendship to Charlie had become very special to her, but because she knew that it couldn't go beyond what they had, she would understand that there would always be a potential love interest along the way. Knowing that he had high standards for relationships, she would never interfere with that in any way. She would always wish the best for him because she knew that his ultimate relationship goal was to get married.

Joey would stop by Parlons once a week. He and Charlie would talk and flirt and have a good time with each other. She would notice little things, like his remarks whenever she had to step away from him to deal with another male customer. He never seemed to like it, but he was always playful with his comments, so she took it in stride. Charlie didn't care for petty jealousies, but she could learn to smile and enjoy lighthearted and playful jealous comments. That's what she considered Joey's remarks to be.

She and Joey would alternate visiting each other at their apartments, weekly. The sex between them was "bananas", because they both had high sex drives, and they both wanted to please each other, and they did. They could hardly get enough of each other, but once a week is what worked for both of them, based on the time they had to spend with each other. The anticipation of sex with each other kept the desire between them high and top of mind.

About four weeks into their affair, Joey accused Charlie of dealing with other men. Charlie had gotten tired of the daily phone calls, usually about nothing, so she asked if he could refrain from calling daily. He did for about a week, then he went back to the daily calls. She would just ignore them if she was busy. This caused Joey to think that she was dealing with other men, but Charlie told him from the beginning that she had other friends. Even though Joey was wrong about Charlie, he didn't have the right to call her out on it, since she was upfront about not wanting to be in a relationship and the fact that she had other male friends.

He and Charlie would continue to have arguments over many of the things that irritated her, mostly his jealousy that he had no right to. She couldn't take it anymore, so she ended their sexual relationship. He would stop calling for a few days, but would then call her with "out of the blue" accusations about what he believed she was doing with other men, while they were dealing with each other. She would continually tell him that even if those things were true, and they weren't, that would be her business and he had no right to be angry about any of it.

He would eventually stop calling, and Charlie would tell herself that she now knew why he was single. He had some real issues that he needed to get therapy for, and she did tell him that during their last phone call. He disagreed, but Charlie felt like she did her job by making him aware that he had some issue that he should get help for. And she told him that he should ask his family if they felt he needed help. She assured him that they would agree that he did.

Family

Today was Charlies moms 78th birthday. Every year her three brothers and herself would make their mothers birthday a big deal. Even though they would always just celebrate at the family home, each of them would buy her a different genre of gifts.

Charlie was catering dinner again this year, but she also bought her mom three complete outfits, including shoes. Jerrell would have a carpet installer come by for his mom to pick out some new wall to wall carpeting for the house, from a swatch book. He also had new living room furniture delivered the day before, that his mother had picked out previously. Taylin gave his mother $1000.00 to spend as she chose, and he would also give her some beautiful diamond earrings and a matching necklace. Her youngest brother, Dennon, would give his mom some gift certificates to be pampered at a spa for the day, and for different massages and facial treatments. These would all be in a huge gift basket that had all kinds of spa products for her to use at home.

This was always a big day for them and their mother, whom they were all very close to. Dad was there too. He had a stroke a few years before, and Charlie would help in getting him a gift to give his wife. Charlie would always pick up the latest perfume set for him to give to her mother, with the lotions and shower gels included. She would buy new towels sets for the master bathroom for him to give her too.

Charlie's dad had always owned his own businesses and wasn't always on the right side of the law, but she respected her father for doing whatever he needed to do to take care of his family. He was also a lady's man who didn't always do right by her mother with his many infidelities over the years. But Charlie loved her father dearly, and she was definitely a daddy's girl. He gave her everything that she could want or need growing up, along with her mother. His stroke left him paralyzed on his left side, so he walked with a cane, and his speech was still impaired. His sons would usually take him wherever he needed to go since he couldn't drive anymore, and Charlie lived further away.

Family and neighbors would come and go most of the day, as they brought gifts and stayed to eat a plate of food and some cake or take some to go. They all loved her mom because her mother was always someone who treated everyone with respect and had a way of making everyone feel special in some way. That part of her mom's personality was truly a gift. Whenever family and friends who had left the neighborhood, came into town, they would always stop to see Ms. Lenore, Charlie's mom.

Whenever Charlie came home, and people were visiting, they would be happy to see her, and would ask her questions about where she lived now, and what she was doing with herself. Charlie didn't mind the questions, and she was flattered that they were even interested. They would make her feel as if they had pride in her success, and she liked that feeling. She would enjoy the discussions and learn about how others in the neighborhood were doing, especially those who were doing well. Whenever someone was into artistic endeavors, she would ask questions so that she could try to connect with them to see if she could carry their art in her consignment shop, or on the walls of Parlons. This was a way for her to give back to her old neighborhood.

There was a shelved wall of pictures in the house that everyone was drawn to. There were family pictures from the time that they were all children, and pictures of family members and friends of family members before they were born. There were also pictures of different people in the neighborhood, and for some reason, everyone loved going to that wall. These weren't all portraits and headshots, many of them were photo's that were taken at different places in the neighborhood or during different years and events. People always got a kick out of seeing someone who they knew during their younger years. The hairstyles and clothes were always a topic of discussion and humor, too.

Memories.

Charlie walked over to the wall of photos and began to reminisce about the good old days. She would see pictures of her and her cousins and remember the fun they had playing street games like kickball, monkey in the middle, truth or dare, red light/green light, and many others. There were pictures of her and her brothers, teaching her how to skate and ride a bike. She would see another picture with family members during the Easter holiday one year, and remember the fun of dying eggs and making Easter baskets, and watching The Ten Commandments until 12 something in the morning.

She saw another picture of her graduation from Junior High school, with her parents on each side of her, and how they always had pride in her academic achievements. That wall brought back many good memories, but not just to her, to everyone who approached it with familiarity.

Then she saw a picture of her uncle, who she remembered reminded her of her father, and she was close to him. He would take her and a couple of her other girl cousins out of town to Charlie's aunts, his sisters, house. Her aunt had three daughters, so, all the girls would have a good time being girly and playing games whenever they were over there. They would always stay for dinner, then leave when it was dark outside; it was a fond memory.

One night, while Charlie and her parents were on vacation in Atlantic City, there was a phone call that her uncle Rollens was shot. They had to pack up and drive home that same night. By the time that they reached home, news was there that he had passed away from his gunshot wounds. This was Charlie's first experience with death, and it really saddened her. She would save her tears for her bedroom, and she did cry hard.

She would overhear that three guys tried to stick her uncle up, but he refused to give up his money, then pulled out his gun. He shot two of the perpetrators, but the third one shot him. One of the thieves died on the spot, but the other lived. Her uncle survived to make it to the hospital, but they weren't able to save him.

The two men involved in his death did less than five years in prison. This was common when it came to a Black life in the hood, back in the 1970's. There was little value put on the life of a Black man.

The next picture that Charlie's eyes fell on, was of her oldest brother and a close friend of his. She remembered Tooney as a funny guy who was always nice to her, and protective of her. One day her brother Jerrell came home upset and loudly exclaimed to everyone in the house that Taylin and Tooney had been shot. The house became in an uproar, as her mother, father, and brother would leave for the hospital. Charlie stayed home with her aunt. Her parents didn't want her at the hospital. By the time that everyone came back home, they let everyone know that Taylin would be fine, but Tooney had passed. Charlie couldn't contain her tears and cried on the sofa for nearly an hour.

She would find out that her brother and Tooney were shooting dice, when one of the guys got mad that he lost, then decided to try to stick up the game. When one of the other guys started pulling out his gun, the stickup guy started shooting wildly as he was running to get away. He shot both Taylin and Tooney in the melee. Taylin was hit in the leg, but Tooney was shot in the abdomen, and the doctors were unable to save him.

Then she saw a picture of her cousin who she was close to, almost like a brother. She began to recall the day when he lost his life. She and Jeff were playing a game of Pat (a card game) when she realized that he was cheating. She got angry with him because she took the game seriously, and they were also playing for money.

It was only a dollar, but she didn't think that it was funny that he cheated, but he did. He told her that he was just having fun and that he didn't even want the couple of dollars that was on the table. She made it clear to him that playing a game with a cheater wasn't fun, and that she wasn't going to play any card games with him ever again. He told her that she was stupid for being angry, and that made her angrier, so she went upstairs to her room and locked her door.

She would lay down on her bed and eventually fall asleep. A couple of hours later, there was a frantic knock on her bedroom door that frightened her. It was her brother Dennon, and he could hardly get the words out, but she heard him say something about Jeff being shot. Her heart dropped, then she ran downstairs to see what was going on. Her mother told her that Jeff had gotten shot by one of his boys and that he was dead.

Charlie couldn't believe what she was hearing. She was in shock, and she couldn't really comprehend that Jeff was dead. It took a while for it to hit her, but when it did she wanted to cry, but she had no more tears. This was the third year of deaths for her, of people who she was close to. And it would prove to be more than her emotions could handle, so they shut down on her.

She had no more tears for anyone. She didn't want to go back upstairs to lay down, so Charlie just sat there with a pillow behind her in the corner of the sofa and stared at the TV. It was on with a TV show playing, but she wasn't watching any of it. It was just a place for her to focus her eyes as she thought about their argument, then thought about the fun that they had over the years.

After Charlie's thoughts returned to the present, she would go upstairs to her old bedroom, and her mind was flooded with memories of how lucky she was. She had a bedroom of her own, when she was a child, with a canopy bed, and a vanity, and her own phone line. She always had beautiful clothes and lots of them. She had beautiful expensive jewelry and watches. Her parents truly gave her everything. Her parents "spoiled" her, although Charlie disliked that term because she was never a little brat who acted like a spoiled child. She was still sweet and quiet, even though her parents gave her everything, at least that's how she remembered it.

Home Sweet Home.

After the yearly festivities to celebrate her mom's birthday, and the cleanup with the help of other relatives and friends, Charlie was finally on her way home. No matter where she would go, and even when she had a great time out, she couldn't wait to get back home to her cozy condo. She truly created a place of peace within her condo, and her bedroom was her solace from the world. Everything about it represented what she loved and enjoyed, and what she needed to bring her peace.

The amber lighting that she used in her lamp by the bed, along with the amber flames of her electric fireplace always created a peaceful atmosphere in her bedroom. Her bookcase with many of her favorite books and her desk with her cherished bankers' lamp were material things that brought her joy. Her desk globe along with her wall portraits of maps, and storage cases, with old world map prints, provided the visual excitement that she appreciated. Her brass high-velocity fan brought her peace throughout the night, with its white noise and constant breeze; she slept well.

Her comforter set along with her matching curtains, and matching bathroom accessories in her master bathroom, provided a warmth of aesthetics that only added to the rest of the peacefulness that her bedroom brought to her and her life.

Charlie was grateful for the ability to have her own place and everything else that she had to bring her peace. Especially after many tumultuous years during her younger years. Followed by the adversities that she faced in her marriage.

New York

New York.

A group of young men came into Parlons. Charlie recognized one of them as a local rapper named Smoke, whose music she was a fan of. She approached him and introduced herself. She let him know that she loved his "From the Streets" CD and she listened to it often. He thanked her, and then he and his boys sat down at a table.

Charlie had Devon take their orders, and apparently, someone had suggested Parlons because Smoke didn't drink, but the rest of the crew did. And they heard that it was a conversation joint, so it was the perfect spot to talk business. Smoke got some coffee and the rest of the crew got some beer. Charlie provided a couple of courtesy hors d'oeuvre and dessert trays, one with an assortment of cheeses and crackers, and another with an assortment of cake and pie slices. The fellas really enjoyed the complimentary snacks and thanked Charlie and Devon when they left. They also left a nice tip, which Charlie told Devon to keep.

The next day, one of the guys from Smoke's crew came in looking for Charlie. She was in the middle of a conversation with a few of her regulars when she saw him come in, so she got up to greet him.

"Hello, how are you today? Back for another round of beer?" Charlie laughed as she attempted to break the ice. He looked so serious.

"No Ms. Charlie, I came back to speak to you."

"Well, how can I help you? First of all, what's your name?"

"You can call me New York."

"Okay, well how can I help you, Mr. New York?"

New York laughed. "No Ms. Charlie, just New York."

"Well, then you have to just call me Charlie, then."

"Okay, that's a deal."

"So, how can I help you?"

"Can we sit down for a minute, to talk?"

"Oh! Sure!" Charlie walked him over to a table, and he pulled out a chair for her to sit in.

"Thank you!", said Charlie.

Then New York sat down and said, "I just wanted to tell you how beautiful I think you are, and I was hoping to possibly get your phone number."

Charlie was taken aback because she knew that he was a lot younger than her, and didn't think he could possibly know her age since he was hitting on her.

"Do you realize that I'm 47 years old? How old are you?"

"Oh! Wow! No, I didn't realize that! Damn! I'm feeling a bit out of my league."

He was feeling a little embarrassed that he didn't recognize how much older she was than him, but finding out that she was older, made her more attractive to him.

"So, how old are you?", asked Charlie.

"I'm 27!"

"Wow! That's young!"

"But I like older women! As a matter of fact, I only deal with older women."

"Yeah, but I'm 20 years older than you. That's a serious age gap."

"I don't think so! I've never dealt with anyone 20 years older than me, but I like you. I like your style, and I think that you're beautiful and sexy. I think your sexiness is what got me. I love me some sexy older women."

Charlie was flattered, but 27? That was a bit too young for her. New York was a 6'3", brown-skinned, average sized young man with a close hair-cut. He had a well-groomed beard and dressed his age in distressed jeans (thank God, they weren't hanging off his bottom, she thought), a nice RL Polo shirt, with some Jordan's (sneakers) on, sporting the colors in his shirt.

"New York, I am quite flattered by your compliments and your charm, but I'm old enough to be your mother."

"Maybe, but you're not my mother. To me, you're just a sexy lady that I'm interested in. I'm not trying to be your man or nothing. I would just like to take you out sometime and show you a good time."

"Once again, I'm flattered, but that's not going to happen."

He seemed really disappointed as he took that statement in, while he stared into Charlie's eyes. She almost felt sorry for him.

"Okay, well I tried. It was really nice talking to you though. I'll still be back. This is a nice place, and I like the view."

He stated that, with eye to eye contact with Charlie, to be clear that she was the view that he liked.

Persistence Pays Off.

New York would stop by Parlons about twice per week, whether he was with his boys, or alone. He didn't let his boys know about his infatuation with Charlie, at least not yet. He would always play it off when they came as a crew, but when he came alone he would try to get her into a conversation with him, just so he could spend time with her since she wouldn't go out with him.

His strategy started to pay off because Charlie was becoming impressed with his knowledge of so many things at such a young age, and his accomplishments. She found out that he was Smoke's producer, and he had lost his parents at a very young age to a tragic accident that left him a multi-millionaire. He was raised by his maternal grandmother, who he was extremely close to. It made sense to Charlie why he was attracted to older women. It was probably because of the void that the death of his mother left.

He was from Brooklyn, New York and learned the music business by being around the industry, and doing whatever he could to help out in any way possible, while in middle school and high school. He picked up all that he could about the industry while hanging around it. He had gone to college and got his MBA, but whenever he had spring break or holiday break, he spent those times around studios.

When he finished his degree, he used his money, his knowledge, and his connections to open his own production studio in Philly. There was enough competition in New York, and Philly always had a lot of talent that was untapped. He knew the city well because he had spent a lot of time in Philly as a youngster, with family who lived there.

New York talked Charlie into coming to his studio, and to watch Smoke do his thing. She went and was very impressed with it, and enjoyed watching Smoke recording some new music. When she was ready to leave, New York walked her to her car, gave her a hug, and stole a kiss. He didn't really steal it because Charlie fell right into it with him.

He was a really good kisser, and Charlie was a bit overwhelmed by it all, and just pulled away from New York and jumped into her car. She did roll down her window and said goodbye before she pulled off. He just waved goodbye to her, no words. He wasn't sure what would happen the next time they saw each other.

He waited a few days before he would go to her café. When he saw Charlie, he didn't know what to expect, but he spoke to her like normal. She spoke to him back, then went over to where he was seated.

"I enjoyed being in your studio the other day. Smoke sounded really good."

"What else did you enjoy?" She just smiled at him.

"What can I get you, New York?"

"Another one of those kisses!" He said it low so that no one would hear him, but Charlie just rolled her eyes up in her head and began to walk away.

"Okay, okay! A slice of sweet potato pie, and some coffee."

Charlie turned around and said, "Thank you!" with the sound of relief in her voice.

"Would you please join me? I want to treat you to the same."

Charlie humored him by joining him. New York changed the subject for the time being and answered some questions that Charlie had about different things she saw at the studio.

New York and Charlie got on the subject of gambling, and Charlie told him that she liked shooting craps, but her thing was roulette. She always came up on roulette and rarely had a loss when she played. So, this was another "in" for New York. Charlie agreed to go to the casino with him so that she could show off her skills. He wanted to go to one of the local casino's, but Charlie still preferred Atlantic City.

Atlantic City.

So, she met him at his studio, because she didn't want folks in her business. He drove to AC in his car, which was a Mercedes Benz convertible. Charlie had a thing for convertibles, and she owned one too; so that was another small win for NY. Although, she wasn't the type of a woman to be swayed by a car because she knew that a car didn't represent a man's character. And many men that she knew with really nice expensive cars were assholes, but it was a nice addition to making for a positive and memorable experience with someone she already liked.

They talked about all kinds of things on the drive to AC. NY was as happy as could be to spend this type of time with Charlie. They did a lot of laughing and talking smack to each other. They decided to go to Caesars because that was Charlie's favorite to go to. They would shoot on the crap tables first, and Charlie did well. NY wouldn't allow her to use her own money, but she won them $5000.00, so NY split it with her. Then they went to play the roulette table. They played for two hours, and once again, Charlie won another $3000.00 for them, so NY split that pot with her too.

Charlie was feeling good with her wins, and from drinking her beer, so when NY asked her to stay over with him at the casino, she felt "why not!" She was really feeling him at the moment, in spite of his age. And since she believed in living in the moment, she went for it. He got them an extravagant suite, which Charlie felt wasn't necessary, but she appreciated it.

NY ordered them room service as soon as they got there. He wanted to light up some weed, but he would wait until room service came so that they didn't report the smell. He and Charlie got comfortable by removing their shoes. He turned on the TV but let Charlie tune into whatever she wanted to see. She wasn't really interested in watching TV, so she turned on a movie that she'd seen many times before so that it didn't distract her.

Once they got their food, they ate and shared each other's dishes. They were really impressed with the quality and flavor of their meals. Once they were done, they both sat back on the bed against the headboard. NY lit up some weed and passed it to Charlie. She wasn't much of a weed smoker, but she was in the moment of it all and wanted to continue her enjoyment of it. They smoked, talked and laughed for a while as their food digested. Then NY leaned into Charlie to kiss on her neck. Then her cheek. Then the side of her lips, because she hadn't leaned into him yet. So, he repositioned himself, so that he could fully kiss her. She grabbed him and kissed him back. She asked if he wanted to jump in the shower with her.

"Fuck no! We can do that shit later! I want you now!"

They both removed their clothes, but NY asked Charlie to leave her underwear on. He enjoyed sex with a woman having a little something on, instead of being fully nude. He told her to pull her breasts out of her bra, so she did. He asked her to get on her knees on the edge of the bed and to face him, and she did. He kissed her as he grabbed her breasts, then he began to suck on them, as Charlie moaned with pleasure.

"I need you to suck my dick, baby." New York whispered in Charlie's ear.

She hesitated but realized that she wanted to do it to him. So, she got off the bed, stood in front of him, then got on her knees. As she performed fellatio on him, he closed his eyes with his head toward the ceiling as he moaned with pleasure.

He whispered, "There's nothing like having a grown ass woman suck your dick."

He didn't want her to stop, but he also wasn't ready to come, so he grabbed her gently to pull her up from the floor. He walked her over to the sofa, took off his boxer briefs, then sat down. He grabbed her hand to guide her to his lap. She removed her panties before straddling him, then grabbed his penis and guided it into her vagina. She just sat on it for a minute while she put her arms around his neck, and began kissing his lips gently. In the middle, on the left side, then on the right side. They then began to kiss with a deep passionate kiss for about a minute, and Charlie started to rock gently in his lap. She then began to move faster, and faster until she had to break the kiss in order to release her screams of pleasure.

She would ride him in his lap, with her knees to the seat cushions. She then came up off him, so that she could reposition her legs so that her feet were against the back of the sofa. She brought them down again as she held on to the back of the sofa, to put him back inside of her. She moaned from the feeling of being so turned on, and his hardness entering her again. She again put her feet to the back of the sofa and rode him, but this time, her position forced him deep inside of her as she delightfully screamed from his length banging on her cervix over and over until she couldn't take it anymore, and fell off of him onto the sofa; panting heavily from being out of breath.

New York positioned her with her back and shoulders to the back of the sofa, and her bottom towards the edge of the seat, and her feet pushed toward her shoulders. His erection was hard enough for him to enter her without the use of his hands since they were being used to pin her legs to her shoulders. He began to bounce on her, so that he would go into her deeply, and come out just enough for the head of his penis to remain inside her. Then he would pump with a constant, steady rhythm that led to an explosive climax for him.

He let go of her legs, but the weight of his body against her in that position, kept her there until he was able to pull himself together. He got up, then went to the bed to lay down. Charlie just sat on the sofa with her eyes closed for a while to enjoy her state for a bit. She ended up falling asleep there. Once NY realized that she wasn't in the bed with him, he went to pick her up from the sofa and laid her on the bed. He laid next to her and fell asleep.

When he awakened in the middle of the night. Her softness was more than he could bear, so he climbed on her from the back. He wanted to make sure that she was awake before he entered her, and she was. Charlie loved the feeling of being awakened to intercourse and couldn't wait to feel him inside of her in such a relaxed mode. He entered her and began pumping slowly. She began to throw her bottom back to him hard, to let him know to give it to her harder. He got the message and began to give her hard slow pumps, then they got faster and faster until she came and came, then he came again intensely from that middle of the night state of not quite asleep, and not quite awake. They both fell back to sleep.

In the morning, when they awakened, NY asked Charlie what she wanted for breakfast, then he got them some room service again. They felt famished and could hardly wait to eat. Charlie jumped in the shower while she waited for the food; NY jumped in with her, wanting to be inside of her one last time before they left. The warm water on their bodies helped to get them both really worked up, so he picked her up so that he could enjoy her against the shower wall. Once again, they had another intensely passionate moment, with a hard release.

Charlie chased him out of the shower so that she could try to finish up. NY jumped out, and just laid on the bed wet until room service buzzed the room. He then put on his underwear and opened the door, as the concierge rolled the cart to the bed. He gave the man a tip before he left. Charlie got out of the shower and put her underwear back on from the night before, she had no choice. They sat and ate their delicious breakfast as they talked about little things in general. Once they were finished, NY took his shower, then got dressed. Charlie had gotten dressed while he was in the shower.

On the way home, they mostly listened to music, and Charlie kept drifting off to sleep, so they didn't talk too much. He took her to her car, then hugged and kissed her, and thanked her for a wonderful night and morning. She thanked him for the same. She drove off to go home and get ready to go to the café.

The Nasty.

Charlie and New York would hang out once or twice a month, and he would continue to stop by Parlons once or twice, weekly. They would have a good time hanging out and going to restaurants, sports bars, cigar lounges, and even strip clubs. They would also go to Atlantic City about once a month and win money every time they would go. And sex was always the cherry on top of a good time. Their sexual connection was deeply erotic, even "nasty" wouldn't be a negative term to describe their sexual fun.

New York loved having sex outdoors, so he would find different spots where they would have sex in places where they could get caught, but never did. At least they never got called out on it. One night after spending time at a strip club, they were both pretty high between the weed that was smoked on the way to the club, and the drinking once they got there. New York had the desire to have sex, so they drove around until they found a warehouse with a parking lot behind it, without too many lights. They found a dark spot near a dumpster.

They sat in NY's car and started kissing as if they were attempting to devour each other's tongues. Their tongues would plunge back and forth as deeply as they could get them, in each other's mouths. Then they would take turns with erratic attempts to suck on each other's tongues, as one would grab hold, then the other would attempt to pull loose, then suck the others tightly, as their tongues battled for dominance. New York would practically climb on top of Charlie to get control of the "kiss" and use his tongue to forcefully lick the inside of her mouth, as their tongues wrestled back and forth. Then she would eventually accommodate his aggressive oral tongue fuck.

While New York was fully engaged in the oral orgy, Charlie was reaching up his shirt to grab, squeeze, twist, and caress his nipples. New York's response was to get out of the car while grabbing Charlie's hand. He then pushed her up against the car and started kissing her again, and aggressively fondling her breasts, then lifting her dress. Charlie was wild with sexual excitement and couldn't wait for him to do whatever he was about to do to her. She didn't care what it was, as long as he kept up his aggression until she received the relief that only his non-stop aggressive sexual behavior would provide.

New York would turn her around to face the car and told her to bend over. She had on the high heels and fishnet stockings that he requested her to wear for him. Charlie loved his requests and enjoyed fulfilling them, knowing the erotic high that doing so gave him, and in return, gave her, knowing that the fulfillment that would occur would be ecstatic. New York would tell Charlie to pull her breasts over her bra, while he snatched her panties and fishnets down to her midthigh. He made her bend over until her back was perpendicular to the car, then he spread her booty enough to allow his erection to slide inside of her.

Charlie's hands were planted firmly against the side of the car, and even though she had on heels, she was still on her toes with her legs spread as wide as she could get them with her panties and stockings at mid-thigh. New

York would tease her vagina by shoving his penis inside her, then pulling it all the way out a few times, until she begged him to "fuck her, and fuck her hard." He kept her bottom spread open as widely as he could while he pounded her vagina with his super hard extremely large member.

As Charlie screamed from the glorious pain, New York told her to "Shut the Fuck Up Bitch, before somebody hears you!" His degrading words made her hotter, as he grabbed her mouth with his huge hand to quiet her screams of painful pleasure. All the aggressive talk and actions that New York was displaying, along with the high that they were feeling, and the fact that they were having sex in a dirty spot near the dumpster, and in a place where they could get caught, caused Charlie to orgasm multiple times before New York would explode his semen all over her back and booty. She could feel it on her and couldn't move until he got some paper towels out of his trunk and cleaned her off.

She held on for dear life while she waited because she surely just wanted to fall out on the ground. She held on, pulled up her panties and fishnets, opened the car door, and fell out onto the back seat. New York couldn't wait to flop in the front seat of his car too. He sat for quite a few minutes with his eyes closed until he felt lucid enough to drive back to the studio, which was 40 minutes away. Charlie remained out on the back seat for the entire ride. He awakened her when they got there to see if she was okay to drive home. She said that she was, but he didn't agree, so he went inside the studio to have one of his boys drive his car to follow him, as he drove Charlie home in her car. He got her inside of her condo, and in bed safe and sound before he left.

The Fight.

New York would call Charlie the next day to make sure that she was okay, and she was. She was getting ready for work, so she didn't talk with him too long. New York would show up at Parlons, later that day to see Charlie and to tell her how much fun he had the night before. Charlie agreed that it was a lot of fun and told him how exciting it was to her. What she didn't tell him was that he was getting a tighter grip on her, with his kinky sexual proclivities, and her deep need to adapt to any kinky sexual circumstance that she was exposed to, with someone she greatly desired.

New York would sit down and wait until Charlie had some time to sit with him. When she did, they started talking about random things, when New York felt comfortable enough to use the word "bitch" to refer to Charlie, as a term of endearment. Charlie understood that was how many people talked to each other in the hood, but she never allowed anyone to call her "bitch" or a bitch outside of sex. She never even let female friends use the term as a term of endearment. She just understood how allowing the term could get out of hand, so she would make it clear to anyone who crossed that line, that she wasn't playing that game with anyone.

New York was a bit irritated by her hardline stance on the word when she encouraged him to use such words during sex. He felt like she was being a hypocrite and contradicting herself. She was very irritated by his lack of understanding about it being okay during sex, but not okay any other time. Her irritation with the conversation was causing her to lose her temper with New York, and the fact that it was at her place of business made it worse. There weren't too many patrons there at the time, but she didn't want it to escalate to where anyone else could hear the conversation, so she asked him to leave.

New York was extremely irritated by her seemingly hypocritical behavior, but he left so that he wouldn't cause a scene, but he surely called her a bitch loud enough for Charlie to hear before he left. This made her furious, but she let him leave, then texted him her disappointment in his behavior. She made it clear that she didn't want to see him again.

Charlie was frustrated that he didn't get the difference between dirty words during sex, and the fact that those words had a different feeling outside of sex; at least to her they did. Maybe it was his age, or maybe she didn't make herself clear, but either way, at that moment, she was done with him. His decision to end their conversation with a clear use of the word as a slur to her was totally disrespectful; he didn't respond back.

New York knew what time she usually got off that day, so he would drive over to the parking garage where she parked her car and waited for her to come out to get into her car. Once he saw her enter the parking garage, he got out of his car before she could get to hers. She wanted no parts of him and told him to get away from her. He tried to apologize and explain to her that he finally understood what she was saying, but all she could think about was his choice to call her a bitch before he left. She jumped into her car, and even though he really wanted to prevent her from doing that, he also knew that it could cause things to end badly at that moment, so he let her leave.

He would continue to stop by the café and text her for the next week, but she ignored him and attempted to stay away from him as much as she could. He would eventually figure out that he needed to give her, her space for a while, so he stopped texting her and stopped coming around. Charlie was relieved and didn't care to see or hear from him again.

Single Again

Charlie received a phone call from Zhon. "I need a story!" She knew from those words that he was single again. He would never call for a story if he were still involved. She was excited and happy to give him what he wanted. The call would almost always end with him wanting to lay back and take a nap, but needing to get ready for work, and her needing to lay back and enjoy the feeling after her mental orgasm. Their needs were fully satisfied simultaneously with phone sex. Neither of them would ever feel any type of emptiness afterward, and there were never any drawn-out conversations following it.

Charlie would later text Zhon to thank him for the phone sex, and he would thank her in return. She would sit back this time and try to figure out why she allowed him to call her whenever he wanted, and always gave him what he wanted. She also needed to understand her attempts to leave him alone after he would get into a relationship, yet could never deny him when he called her after those relationships ended.

She began to realize how much she truly enjoyed him, more than anyone she had ever been with. She wasn't looking for a relationship, so she didn't need any set rules about their friendship. The only thing that she really required was a respect for her, and a respect for her time. He gave her those things. The sporadic nature of their cyber-sex and physical sex made the sex between them scarce, exciting, and highly desired. Their sexual connection was intense for Charlie, and Zhon's aggressive sexual nature matched her need for aggressive sex.

She had come to understand that she needed his aggression on a deeply primal level. With her being a good girl growing up; then her marriage to a man whom she adored; his descent into becoming overprotective, obsessive and controlling; who would eventually emotionally abuse and neglect her, while constantly cheating on her; these things practically destroyed her self-esteem.

When she finally left him, she was emotionally numb. So, when she got involved with another man, she just needed to feel sexy and pretty and desired again. She knew that she wasn't any good for anyone at that point in her life because she was emotionally devoid. All she needed was those things from a man to help her to rebuild her self-esteem, and the pleasure of good sex to bring her out of her emotional dungeon.

Over the years, she would bed quite a few men, something that she never believed in before, but life taught her that much of what she believed before her marriage was just fairytales. She would exercise her sexual freedom, and she enjoyed the reaction that men had to her. Their reaction gave her power, but she was always careful about who she dealt with, and of her reputation. On top of that, once she interacted more with people and the world, she understood her own unique and unordinary qualities as special, and these things helped to rebuild her self-esteem and personal strength.

She believed that these things were the catalyst to cause her to need the aggression that Zhon gave her during sex, with his domineering sexual proclivities. She loved his aggressiveness in a way that caused her sexual interactions with him (physically or otherwise) to leave her in a higher state of ecstasy than anyone could take her. She wanted him to punish her with spankings and to use words that let her know that she was a bad or naughty "bitch."

His physical and verbal punishments would satisfy the need to be reprimanded for the actions that were against her purest moral nature growing up. His strong piercing words would help to confirm her transition from the soft good girl of her youth, to the strong sexual vixen she had become. This was all a subconscious need to balance her moral compass as the good girl who believed that she could be with one man for the rest of her life, with the woman of desire who loved every bit of the sex she had with her male friends, with no regrets.

A second understanding for her was the fact that she wasn't really a fighter when she was younger. Fighting was something that she had no interest in, and she would be one of the only kids who wouldn't hang around to watch an announced or unannounced fight after school. She was uneasy around any type of verbal or physical altercations and preferred not to witness any, and she never really got into any altercations herself. Her shy, quiet nature never gave anyone cause to start trouble with her, and even if that weren't the case, her family was notorious and very protective of her.

So, Charlie believed that she also needed the sexual aggression to force her into a tougher state of mind and physical being, to stand against any type of physical altercation; something that she avoided in her youth. The pain that she experienced during sex with Zhon, and the tolerance that she built up after every encounter, helped her to welcome the potential pain of a physical altercation. Now, instead of walking away from it, she would embrace it, because the adrenaline rush of a painful interaction, would release a desire to inflict pain on her opponent, with the expectation of receiving pain in return. This would no longer be something to run from, but to revel in.

She also realized that a day hadn't gone by that she didn't think about Zhon, since the day that they met. She tried to understand what that was about. Zhon had many personal qualities that she had never witnessed in any man of her past. Qualities that she never thought any man that she would be attracted to would have, and that a man with those qualities would never be able to accept or handle the free-spirited personality that she evolved to. But Zhon was all of this, and still maintained a friendship with her, even knowing and witnessing her dark-side. She believed that it may have intrigued him.

Charlie would often fight with herself about her feelings for him. She didn't understand why she felt so deeply about him, but her thoughts today were helping her to get there.

Lowell

Sweet Music.

Charlie was in the midst of a conversation when a new patron came in and wanted some imported beer that wasn't out in the café. She sent her assistant down to the cellar to get the Stella Artois. When she came back, Charlie waited on the gentleman who requested it. He kept locking eyes with her, but she just kept waiting on him. She had to turn her back to him to ring him up, and when she turned back to give him his change, he said –

"God made you perfectly!"

"Wow! Thank you!" Charlie believed in thanking a compliment as genuine unless there was some negativity that followed it; even if there were ulterior motives.

"You're beautiful, sorry for staring."

"Thank you! No problem! I like men who appreciate women."

The gentleman got his beer and took a seat. He was alone and seemed to need a few moments of relaxation. He couldn't take his eyes off Charlie, so she decided to grab a beer and go sit down and talk with him.

"So, what brings you to Parlons?"

"I was in the area, and figured I'd stop in for a drink."

"So, you're a walk-in or have you heard of us before?"

"I guess you can say that I'm a walk in. I never heard of this place before."

"Cool, well I hope that you find it a place to suggest to others," Charlie smiled.

"Maybe I don't want others to enjoy what I'm enjoying."

"Would that be looking at me? I couldn't help but notice it," Charlie giggled as she said it.

"What is your name by the way?" Charlie extended her hand, "I'm Charlie!"

"My name is Lowell!" He grabbed her hand and kissed it.

"Well, well, well, aren't you a charmer!"

Charlie was, so far, impressed by this hulk of a man, who was well dressed and smelled delicious. He was about 6'4", and a big teddy-bear, who she could just wrap herself in. He was light-skinned, with his hair cut close on the sides, with some natural textured twists on top. She just loved natural hairstyles, and his fit him well. He was her kind of handsome, wore glasses and had a nerdy air about him. Not in an awkward way, but in an intellectual way. She loved intelligence in men.

"So, what do you do, if you don't mind me asking?", Charlie asked.

"Not at all! I'm a music instructor and musician, in town for a gig."

"Nice! What do you play?"

"I play several instruments, including the guitar and the sax."

"Oh, no! Don't tell me that! I *love* the sax! I want to learn to play myself."

"Oh, would you now!" Lowell smiled from ear to ear. "When shall the lessons start?"

Charlie laughed, "Now, now! I appreciate the initiation, but I just met you, sir. Besides, I have a lot on my plate at the moment, so now isn't a good time anyhow."

"Okay, but when you're ready, here's my number." Lowell gave Charlie his business card.

"Why thank you! I'm going to get back to my discussion over here if you don't mind. As a matter of fact, why don't you join in? The more, the merrier!" So, he did.

All That Jazz!

Lowell would make Parlons an everyday event while he was in town, and he thoroughly enjoyed the intellectual conversations of the shop's patrons. Charlie became very impressed and enamored by him, after being in town for a week. He was going home and back to work in Princeton, New Jersey in a couple of days, so he invited Charlie to come watch him play, and to have a lovely dinner before-hand, at the venue. Charlie was delighted and said yes.

When she got to the jazz lounge, Charlie texted Lowell to let him know that she was there. He came outside to meet her and to take her to her seat, but when he saw her, as usual, he couldn't take his eyes off her. She had no idea that he was just standing and staring at her because she was checking her phone for a response from him, then a text from someone else popped up, so she was answering it.

Charlie had on a form-fitting dress that just clung to her perfect curves. It was an electric blue dress, with a low draped back, and was quite kind to her cleavage. It showed just enough that Lowell couldn't stop his eyes from dropping back to stare at it, after looking at the whole package that enveloped Charlie. She loved wearing how high-heeled pumps because they made her feel sexy, and they helped her become taller to be at a closer height to her usually tall lovers.

Once he got his temporary fill of Charlie, he walked over to her, grabbed her hand to kiss it, then hugged her gently with a light kiss on the cheek.

"Well, hello beautiful! What are you trying to do to me, in that dress? Sheesh!!!"

Charlie smiled and said, "I had to represent, right? I can't be showing up at your place of work looking any less than someone who would look good on your arm, could I?

And thank you for your kind compliment. I do appreciate it."

Lowell grabbed her arm and walked her into the building. He introduced her to a few people on the way to their table. The interior of the lounge was very modern and had an exciting atmosphere to it. They sat down to eat before Lowell had to get on stage to play.

When everything was over, Charlie knew that Lowell probably had to hang back to get some things done, so she looked for him to thank him and to wish him goodnight. The band members knew that he had company and didn't want him to have to worry about any wrap-up.

"I'm about to leave but I wanted to thank you for a wonderful dinner, and I really enjoyed your playing along with your band members."

"You're most welcome, but I'm about to leave too. I was hoping that you would accompany me to the condo that I'm staying in while I'm here. I would love to spend some more time with you. I'm gonna hate for this night to end."

"Me too! And I would love to accompany you to the condo."

The Condo.

When they got to the building, the condo was on the fifth floor. When they entered, the lights automatically turned on, and Charlie was very impressed by the place. It was all white, with red, black and white accents. The walls were white, with paintings, portraits, and wall art in red, black and white. The furniture was white Italian leather, with red, black, and white throw pillows. The coffee table and end tables were glass and chrome, with red lamps and black, red and white knick-knacks and accessories on the tables. The wall to wall carpet was white, with throw rugs that were red, black and white. This was the theme of the entire condo, and she just loved it.

Lowell turned on some nice Jazz and offered Charlie something to drink. She asked for some Cabernet Sauvignon. He brought the bottle of wine over to the coffee table, along with her filled glass. Lowell decided to drink some cognac, so he chose some Courvoisier XO Imperial.

"Would you mind if I smoked a cigar? We can sit out on the balcony," said Lowell.

"No, I don't mind at all, and I hope that you have one for me."

Lowell gave Charlie the side-eye, "You smoke?"

"I sure do!"

They went out onto the balcony with their drinks and cigars and closed the glass doors behind them. There was a nice little bistro set out there with an umbrella over the table. He lit the torch lamps to make it feel a bit more atmospheric. He made sure that they sat together at the table and not on opposite sides. There was a hidden speaker that allowed them to hear the music with the glass doors closed. It was a nice warm night, and Charlie had always loved the experience of a warm summers night. There was just something magical about it to her. Even when she drove her convertible in the night air, it gave her such a freeing feeling.

When they got up to go back into the condo, Lowell told Charlie to leave everything on the table. Once inside, as she walked toward the sofa, he grabbed her hand and gently pulled her toward him until she was facing him and in his arms; she hugged him at his waist. He looked down at her as they swayed back and forth in rhythm to the music.

"*My* you're beautiful!"

"Thank you. You're not so bad yourself," she said softly as she looked up at him.

"I want you really badly."

"I know, I can tell," She smiled, as she felt his hardness pressing on her.

"Can I have you?"

"Every bit of me!"

"You know that I'm married," he softly stated it instead of asking a question, although it was an attempt to make that clear before doing anything.

"I know..., I saw the ring at dinner tonight." She was hoping that the conversation stopped there so as not to ruin the mood. She had come to terms with dealing with a married man a few years ago. She didn't chase men, so if he came after her, and she had a connection with him, she wasn't going to deny herself the experience of him, even if she found out he was married. She wasn't looking for a relationship anyway, and this fit right into her lifestyle. Sporadic sex and companionship, with no emotional hang-ups, and unrealistic expectations. Him being married gave her a clear and defined picture of what to expect.

She also had no interest in knowing about his home life. Whatever their relationship became, it was only about him and her for the amount of time they spent together during that moment. Once it ended, nothing else was any of her business, and what she did was none of his.

Charlie was about living life and learned to appreciate the special moments in life. She never took them for granite. And she never left home seeking any type of relationship, she just allowed life to happen. Whoever she met during her day, she met; and hoped that she would have a positive effect on anyone she encountered. And any initial encounter would determine the next encounter. She didn't date, so every encounter with a person would determine where they placed in her life, whether that would be a passing stranger, or an associate, or friend, or lover.

So, that conversation did end there, and Charlie and Lowell began to kiss, and they kissed passionately. While they were kissing, Lowell began to help Charlie out of her dress. He would break from the kiss when necessary. While she was still in her underwear, he told her not to move, then he began to take off his clothes while enjoying looking at her in her sexy lingerie.

Once he was nude, he asked Charlie if she minded taking her underwear off while he watched. She didn't mind at all. She liked watching his expressions as her breasts fell out of her bra, once she opened the back, and allowed it to fall to the floor. She intentionally kept on her shoes, as she turned around with her bottom towards Lowell, while she bent over to pull her panties down, then removed them. She would bring them to her face as she covered her nose and mouth to inhale her own scent.

"Mmmm…," said Charlie.

Then she threw her panties to Lowell for him to enjoy her scent. He closed his eyes as he took a deep breath into her panties and enjoyed the smell of her juices and perfume; his erection became stiffer. Lowell threw her panties on the sofa, and just took in her beauty; he was overwhelmed by her delicious curves. He just wanted to devour her.

He led her into the bedroom, which was pretty spectacular too. The same music was playing in there, and there was a beautiful artificial fireplace on the wall, and the room lights were dim. He pulled back the covers on the bed, for her to lay down. He got over top of her and hovered as he kissed her some more. Then he grabbed her breasts and began sucking on them. This had her moaning and writhing as she grabbed the pillows from beneath her head and threw them on the floor. She preferred to lay flat while on her back during sex; it amplified the pleasure for her. She began grabbing the sheets as his gentle sucks drove her wild.

He then went down between her legs and began to kiss her groin area, then her vaginal area, then he spread the lips to her vagina and gently got her clitoris between his lips. He then used his tongue and lips to pleasure her. She tasted delightful to him. He put two of his fingers inside of her vagina while he orally satisfied her. He manipulated her vagina and clitoris until she climaxed. Her orgasm was intense, so he left her alone for a few minutes to pull herself together.

While he was leaving her be, he was stroking himself so that he didn't lose his erection. Once Charlie recovered, she took over and stroked his penis for him. She then kissed it and began kissing his belly and his nipples. While his erection was under her belly, she started sucking on his left nipple, while rubbing and flicking his right one. When she felt like he had enough, she went back down to his groin area and grabbed his penis. She began kissing on each side of his thighs while his erection was in her hand. She then began to lick on his scrotum, then gently sucked it into her mouth. She used her tongue to explore it while in there, then gently released it from her mouth.

She began sucking on his penis and took the entire length into her mouth. She then came back up to the tip, then took it all the way into her mouth again. She did this several times, then got up to sit on it. She got it inside of her and moaned as she did it. It felt wonderful inside of her. She lightly bounced up and down on it a few times, then she began to ride it back and forth. She got into a good rhythm and he was super-hard inside of her, so she began to scream loudly with pleasure. He wanted her to enjoy herself and get another release before he got his. When she fell off him, he knew that she got what she needed, so now it was his turn.

Charlie was already on her back, so Lowell got on top of her and inserted himself into her. He pumped a few times then pulled out. He grabbed her legs and put them over his shoulders. He then bounced himself so that his member went in and out of her several times. This drove her crazy as it aroused her again, quickly. He then began pumping at a steady pace, and Charlie told him "harder".

This excited him even more, so he obliged her. She began to scream with pleasure and said "harder"… "faster". So, he gave her what she wanted. He didn't want to climax, but he did, and he climaxed hard. He laid on her for a few minutes until he got himself together. Then he rolled over to lay on the side of her.

"Mmm, mmm, mmm, you are quite tasty in every way. I really enjoyed you!"

"Does that mean that we're done for the night?"

Charlie and Lowell were on their sides facing each other when Charlie asked the question.

"Not if you're planning to stay, so are you?"

"If you want me to I will, but I don't want to make any assumptions."

"I would love it if you spent tonight with me."

"Awesome!"

Charlie leaned into him to start kissing him again. She enjoyed the feeling of her skin touching his, and they were definitely intertwined. She was enjoying the sensual energy from the skin to skin contact. It was almost as if she could feel a slight charge going through her when her naked skin touched his. The same charge that she usually felt when she was nude with her lover, and their skin touched. She wanted to give him enough time to be able to regroup, so she laid back to allow him to initiate when the time was right for him. She was aware that the refractory period on average was about 30 minutes but also realized that all men were different. They had sex two more times that night.

The next morning, Charlie got up to use the restroom, and she washed up a little just in case they had sex again that morning. She jumped back in the bed to take a little nap until Lowell awakened. When he did, he pulled her over to him and helped her on her side with her back to him. He penetrated her from the back with his stiff erection. She jumped and winced a bit from the soreness of the night before and the size of his stiffness. He could tell that she was a bit sore, so he was slow and gentle with her. But she disliked slow and gentle and told him to "Fuck me hard!"

"I don't want to hurt you, I can tell that you're sore."

"Fuck me hard! My soreness isn't an issue, but my pleasure is. I need you to fuck me
hard so that I can climax from the pain and the pleasure. That's what I want and that's what I enjoy."

So, Lowell pumped her hard and fast, as she screamed with enjoyment as he aggressively satisfied her. Her revelation turned him on even more, so that put him in an animalistic mode. He sexed her in many positions, on the bed, and off the bed, and finally had her stand on her toes, bent over the side of the bed and pounded her · hard and fast until he came. He could tell that she had come, but he didn't know that she came several times from his aggression.

They both laid on the bed out of breath and very satisfied. They fell back asleep for about an hour before getting up and taking their showers. Lowell made Charlie some breakfast and gave her one of his shirts to sit and eat before she got dressed in her clothes from the night before and went home. She really enjoyed herself with him and would think of their night together, off and on for the next week.

He stopped into the Parlons before he left to go back home. She thanked him again for a wonderful evening and told him to make sure that he stopped by when he was back in town. He told her that he would give her a call sometime during the week, and she said okay. It wasn't a big deal to her either way because she knew that she wouldn't call him, given his marital status, but she would respond if he called or texted. She figured that she'd just see him the next time that he was in town.

Parlons Café

Let's Talk.

Parlons was Charlie's baby! This represented the essence of who she was. An intelligent Black woman, who needed conversation to help her to grow; intellectually, spiritually, socially, and politically. She also needed that human connection of being face-to-face with the people who she was communicating with. She had enough of social media and its endless conversations on the same subjects, with no resolutions. She no longer wanted to get excited about great ideas and movements, only for them to get started, then fizzle out; or to never get started at all.

She met great people though and was able to have enlightening and spirited conversations, which allowed her to express herself, to vent, to debate, to learn, and to grow from the people who she interacted with. She also got the chance to go to different events to actually meet many of the people who she befriended on social media. She made friendships that she knew would last a lifetime. Friendships that would never have happened without social media, because she wasn't a very social person, and she definitely wouldn't have walked in the same circles of her newfound friends. There were only a few who she connected with on a level of understanding, relatability and comfort, but she met many who she liked and respected for their intelligence, wisdom, and accomplishments in their fields of expertise.

Charlie had gotten to the point where she felt she could no longer grow from social media, and it was becoming more of a nuisance than a pleasure. The endless conversations on the same subjects; the ignorant memes that people would believe just because they existed; the lack of research before commenting or believing someone just because they liked and respected them. The list was becoming too long as to why she shouldn't be on there, then why she should. It was time for her to delete her account. Deactivating was no longer the solution for her because she had no more interest in interacting in a virtual environment anymore; at least not on Facebook.

So, one day she just deleted her account. No saving of pictures or phone numbers or conversations, or even things that she saved in her inbox to read later. She had no desire to spend one more day on Facebook, so she went through everything that was necessary to permanently delete her account, and it felt good to her. She would now have more time to live life in reality, instead of giving up so much of her time in a virtual reality.

Charlie wanted to make plans with her friends to have dinner and just talk about anything and everything. She had so much to talk about and wanted feedback and pushback from friends who could help her to think deeper about her subjects of interest. But she realized that she couldn't always line up her free time with the free time of those friends who she wanted to converse with. She owned a few properties on the outskirts of Philly and had a consignment shop and a boutique that was attached to her third property that use to be a bar. She didn't want to use it as a bar, but couldn't figure out what to do with it.

So, one day when listening to an audiobook, "At the Existentialist Café", the idea came to mind as to what she wanted to do with the bar. She would make a coffee, tea, wine, and beer bar out of it; with an atmosphere of communication. She needed a name for her place, so she dropped the words Let's Talk into her translator, and the French translation for let's talk was parlons. It was perfect for the name of a café, and it was French, which was the central place of the audiobook.

She wanted the interior to represent her and all things artistic, so she came up with a plan and design, with a friend who was a carpenter, to redesign the bar to represent what she wanted the café to be, and the end result was perfect to her. She also had art from local artists and people who she knew that made art. So, she hung them on the walls with price tags for her patrons to purchase if they saw one that they wanted. She kept the overflow in her consignment shop next door and would suggest to her customers to stop over there to check them out.

She had hors d'oeuvres and other snacks that were made fresh daily, by different local home cooks and bakers, along with those who she knew personally from her hometown community. She had homemade cakes slices, cupcakes, pies, and other desserts. She also had different types of bread to toast for patrons who enjoyed toast with their tea or coffee. She would change up her menu daily so that she didn't have to have too many varieties on hand each day.

She wanted to celebrate cultural diversity, so she would have hors d' oeuvres and pastries from different countries each week on her menu. This week it may be German hors d'oeuvres and pastries, then next week it may be Spanish hors d'oeuvres and pastries. This would be in addition to her regular snacks.

She decided not to celebrate any holidays at the café, with decorations and holiday greetings, because she wanted all to be and feel welcome no matter what day it was. She would respond to any holiday greetings from her customers, out of respect for their own personal celebrations. She would close on Dr. Martin Luther King Jr.'s holiday as a day of service for her, Devon, and those who worked for her part-time, as a personal decision out of respect for the holiday and what it took to get it. She would also close on Thanksgiving and Christmas, more for her employees, than because she needed off. She knew that for many, these were days to be with family. She had also learned that it wasn't worth being open because although the café didn't celebrate the holidays, there usually wasn't enough of a turnout to make it feasible to open on those holidays.

Charlie was more about helping people than she was about the capitalist attitude of making a profit, over the loyalty to the people. She greatly disliked the way that companies now discarded people with experience, to hire people who cost them less money to do the same job, incompetently. There was no longer any loyalty to the people who helped create and build a company; the loyalty was only to the almighty dollar. She understood why, but she despised it.

So, with owning her own businesses, all she wanted was to grow them into self-sustaining businesses that would allow her to live comfortably, without the need to work for someone else. If she were to become rich, it would have to be through her investments. She wasn't willing to sell out what she created, for the sake of a profit. This was her life and purpose; this was her legacy.

Why Are You Single?

"Why are you single?"

A fairly new patron had been checking out Charlie for the past couple of weeks. He'd been asking questions about her to some of the regulars to find out if she was available. He couldn't understand why a woman who he felt should have been scooped up and married at her age, would still be single; something had to be wrong with her. He *was* very interested in her, but he was leery based on his experiences. Women who seemed so perfect had to have some deep issues if they were still single in their 40's (He knew her age because he asked, and the other patrons told him. Charlie was very honest about her age and had no qualms on revealing it). So, he decided to ask Charlie himself, why she was single. Why did he do that?

"Why am I single?", Charlie repeated with an attitude. She disliked that question because she already knew that men who asked that question usually had assumptions. But she would quickly drop the attitude to enlighten the gentleman, either to dispel his belief about older single women or to piss him off to insult his ignorance to her own personal answer; however, he perceived it.

"I'm single because I choose to be single."

"And why would a beautiful woman who seems to have everything going for her, choose to be single."

"Because I like my freedom."

"What does that mean? Don't you want to be married at some point?"

"I've been married before and don't see the need to do it again."

"Why?"

"Because it's not necessary. I'm not having any children, so I don't see the need to be married. Besides, marriage was created at a time when women couldn't make a living for themselves. Women depended on men for survival, so marriage guaranteed that, as a legal contract, and/or a religious commitment. And living in a mostly patriarchal world, we were also at the mercy of men. If you had a good man as a husband, it was a blessing.

But if you had a husband who saw you as his property instead of as his partner, you were usually in trouble. These types of men felt as though if they took care of home, they could do what they wanted, and they did. Some of these men had no care or respect for their wife's feelings, so this caused these women much emotional pain, but women always endured. And some women would be abused physically and sexually by their husbands, because they didn't respect their wives as partners, and saw them as property, as I've mentioned before.

These women had no real recourse because men controlled everything, so trying to reach out for help fell on deaf ears. Even some families felt like this is how it is, deal with it, so women continued to endure. Getting a divorce wasn't an answer for many, because who would take care of them and their children. Even if a woman could get a job, it usually wouldn't pay enough to be able to live off of, with their needs met, along with their children; so, women stayed in marriages to men who treated them badly.

Fast forward to today, and we no longer have to get married, nor do we have to stay in bad marriages. We can make our own money and live a comfortable life even if we have children. It was a hard, long road through history to get here, but we finally got here, and I am grateful to all the women who have fought for our rights. We still have a way to go for full equality, but we are getting there. And for the record, this is our time; please understand that.

This is our time to lead and shine, so if we want to do that without a partner, then that's our choice. If we wish to do it with a partner, that's our choice too. Something that we didn't really have in the not so distant past. Something that I am grateful for, and I am exercising my right to choose to be single instead of pairing myself in a lifelong relationship with someone out of a financial need to be taken care of. Does that answer your question?"

"Uh, yeah, I guess it does!" She gave the gentleman plenty to think about, and he left her alone, at least for the moment.

The Threesome.

"Oh, Shit!!!"

Charlie was behind the back counter getting some drinks when Zhon walked in the door. She was entertaining Lowell who was seated at a nearby table.

"What, what's wrong?" Asked Devon.

Charlie kept her relationship with Zhon private, so she just told Devon that she had forgotten to get something, but she had no idea that Zhon was coming to town. Charlie's heart dropped. Zhon saw her in the back and smiled at her, as he walked toward her. Charlie came from behind the counter and met him right before he got to the table where Lowell was. Lowell saw everything because he loved looking at Charlie. He gathered what was going on, but was as cool as could be. Charlie walked Zhon to Lowell's table and introduced them.

"Lowell, this is Zhon, a good friend of mine. And Zhon, this is Lowell, a good friend of mine too."

The men shook hands and felt Charlie's nervousness. Zhon asked Lowell if he minded if he sat at his table. Lowell welcomed him. Charlie started walking away after she introduced the men, and as she walked away, she smacked the middle of her face with an open hand, looking toward the back wall. She wasn't sure what to do, but when she finally calmed down, she realized that both men knew that she had another lover. Once she rationalized the situation, she felt in control again, then went back to the table. She gave Lowell his drink and brought over some iced tea for Zhon.

Both men were at ease, talking about the Nate Parker controversy, and that also took them into a conversation about the Bill Cosby case. Charlie decided to join in on the conversation because she had a lot of thoughts and opinions about both.

"Well, I'll tell you this… What I am noticing, is that many women don't have the tolerance for anything that even looks like rape. We are finally coming into our own power and we are using it to right the wrongs that have been perpetrated against us through history. So, the women who have experienced rape, who have had to witness the aftermath of what a rape victim goes through, or who has been the support system of a rape victim, don't have any interest in attempting to understand any situation where a woman is in no condition to unequivocally consent to sex.

I'm able to see things a little more objectively because I come from a family of many men, I have never been raped, and I have never had to be the support system of a rape victim. But my advice to men is to never attempt to have sex with any woman who cannot give an unequivocal yes to the idea of sex of any kind. One-night stands need to become an interaction of the past. Having sex with someone who you don't know, puts you in a very precarious position. A position that can affect the rest of your life and this goes for men and women. Times are changing, and we are in positions where we as women can fight for and protect other women now.

Patriarchy is on its way out, and even though the justice system is still male-dominated, we are slowly gaining the power that we need to make justice for women a more realistic outcome in cases where men cannot relate to what we go through, in many instances of crime. Some of these lawyers and judges surely see themselves in some of these men, and see their actions as causing harm, unintentionally. And even at times blaming the women for what has happened to them.

It's time for women to educate those men who think that it's okay to force themselves on women when we are confused, intimidated, inebriated, afraid, or even just naïve, that it's never okay to have sex with us without a clear message that it's what we want. If you're not positive that sex is consensual, then it *should not happen*. And if you choose to not exercise your own self-control, then you are setting your own self up for some unwelcomed consequences."

The guys listened with a full understanding of what Charlie was saying, and their respect for her and her thoughts gave them information that they could surely pass on to others in conversation. Her insight didn't resolve all their thoughts and opinions on both controversies, but she surely provided an understanding that gave both men food for thought, and words to relay to others.

Lowell got up to leave so that he could go to the lounge to play for the evening. He and Zhon shook hands and thanked each other for a good conversation. Charlie walked him out of the café, then they hugged and kissed each other on the cheek.

"You okay?", said Lowell.

"Yeah… That was a bit awkward at first, but then I realized that I've always been honest with you both about my lifestyle."

"Yes, you have… I enjoyed you last night and this morning." Lowell said in a soft "I'm going to be missing you today" voice.

Charlie looked into his eyes and said, "I really enjoyed you too, like always."

They gave each other another quick hug, then parted ways. When she came back in, she sat with Zhon and took a deep breath.

"You looked a bit stressed there for a minute." He started laughing. Charlie looked at him with her mouth twisted, then said…

"I was for a minute or two until I realized that you two weren't a surprise to each other."

"No, you've always been straight up."

"Well, I appreciate how well you both handled that. You took a lot off my shoulders at that moment..." "You really caught me off guard!"

"I apologize for that. I wanted to surprise you."

"Yeah, well, you surprised me alright." They both started laughing.

"It all worked out fine. You handled your business the right way, so no drama here, babe." Charlie just smiled.

"So, what are you doing in town?"

"I came home to visit the family."

"Is everything okay?"

"Yes! All is well!"

"So, am I going to get to spend some time with you?" she said in a sweet sexy voice. Zhon knew what that tone meant. "When are we fucking?"

"I wouldn't have it any other way. What're you doing tonight?"

"Nothing, but, um..." She didn't know how to tell Zhon that she and Lowell were intimate that morning, but she found the words.

"Um, I was with Lowell this morning."

"And???"

"Well, I didn't want you to be blindsided by that. You might want to wait at least a couple of days. How long are you here for?"

"For the week, but we're not waiting for shit. I'm fucking that pretty ass tonight. I don't care who you fucked this morning."

Charlie's eyes got wide, then she was thoroughly turned on by the thought of being with two men on the same day. In her mind, she called herself a nasty hoe, then giggled to herself. She wasn't sure why she was so turned on by the idea, but she was. And Zhon's lack of jealousy and his lack of concern baffled her and turned her on at the same time. This was one of those times when she didn't need to understand, and just wanted to enjoy the experience. And the excitement had her heart pounding; she couldn't wait till tonight.

Charlie believed in helping to create a pleasant experience for herself and the person whom she shared her moments with. She understood how lasting, good memories were; and how they improved a person's happiness. The more good thoughts and memories you have to dwell on, the more positive your life's experience becomes. And those pleasant thoughts can help you through bad times, stressful times, and through boring times.

So, whenever her experience with another was in her possession, she did the little things that were in her power, to make it as pleasant as she could for herself, and her companion. She would always make sure that she looked good and smelled good, and that her condo was neat and clean. Not that she didn't always do these things, but instead of waiting to wash her hair tomorrow, she would just do it today. Instead of tidying up her living room tomorrow, she would make sure that it was done today. Little things like that.

During her time of self-healing in the past, she learned the importance of affecting all the senses. This was especially important to mental health while dealing with depression. So, this carried over into her special moments with friends. She would make sure that she looked good, and her condo was neat and clean; to affect his sense of sight. She would make sure that she smelled good and that her home smelled good, to affect his sense of smell. She would make sure that her kisses, her body, and her vagina would taste clean and pleasant. She would make sure that her body was soft and smooth to his touch.

These things came naturally to her, after understanding them and living this way for so long. She understood the importance of these things to her own experiences too, so she also did these things for herself. The experiences with her friends were her experiences too, and these would be her memories to dwell on as well.

She would pick out a sexy dress, and even though she normally wore matching underwear, she would always make sure that she wore her prettiest sets when she had company. She knew the cliché that men were visual creatures, and she also knew that having on any type of memorable outfit or underwear made the memory of the experience more lasting; for her and for him. Especially if *he* was taking any of it off her.

When she felt like she looked pretty and sexy, she felt pretty and sexy. And she also had a confidence that she projected, which was a very attractive characteristic to the type of men she preferred. She liked men who genuinely liked and respected women. Men who wouldn't be offended by another man enjoying her beauty, as long as they didn't do it in disrespect. She liked men who trusted her to handle a situation before they just jumped into it, but they would be watching and listening for any sign of blatant disrespect that needed male interference. That was a rare occurrence for Charlie, for she usually handled any negative situation like the powerful woman that she was. Pain and adversity taught her well.

When Zhon got to her place, she buzzed him up. She opened the door slightly before he got to her apartment so that he could just come in. She stood in the middle of the floor so that he would see her once he opened the door all the way. She was wearing a red wrap dress that accentuated her curves, and showed full cleavage, with black patent leather heels.

As Zhon looked at her from head to toe, she pulled the ties on her dress and allowed it to fall open. Zhon's excitement was visible, as she allowed the dress to roll off her shoulders and arms, and drop to the floor. This exposed the black lace bra and panties that she had on under the dress. The contrast of the black to her caramel colored skin provided him with a feeling of a sexy piece of art coming to life.

Her bra fit perfectly around her bosoms, with them being pushed together like two perfect mounds, and the scallops of the cups decorating them for visual consumption. Then her panties fell below her sexy navel in a slight V-shape, as they hugged her full hips and exposed her thick thighs with their thigh-high cut.

Zhon walked over to her, grabbed her face and kissed her intensely. He then turned her toward the sofa and told her to bend over the side. He unbuckled his belt, unzipped his fly, then pulled his pants down to his ankles. He dropped his boxers to expose his erection, then pushed the crotch of Charlie's panties to the side, as he slid himself inside of her and pounded her with no mercy.

"So, you gave my pussy away to that muthafucka this morning, huh?"

"Yes..." She could barely get the word out, as she was shouting with pleasure.

"Did I tell you that you could give my pussy away?"

"No baby!"

"So, what do think I should do to you for being disobedient!" Zhon pulled out of her, knowing that this would displease Charlie.

"Baby, stop playing! I need you to finish!"

Zhon was no longer behind her when she turned around, he had gone into the bedroom. Charlie went into the bedroom, and Zhon was naked on the bed. She ran over and jumped on him, strategically, so that she didn't hurt his "parts".

"Why'd you do that? I need you to finish!", said Charlie.

She was straddling him, and face to face as she softly asked the question before she passionately kissed him. He smacked her bottom pretty hard, as she kissed him, and it just turned her on more.

"Is that all you got baby?" She said softly and erotically.

Zhon made a motion to get up, so Charlie rolled off him. He told her to remove her bra, and to come to the side of the bed. She still had on her panties and heels, and she did as she was told. Zhon located his belt and put it in front of her on the bed so that she knew what he was about to do. Her heart was racing with excitement. Her lack of response let him know that what he was about to do was okay with Charlie. While she was eyeing the belt, he took the opportunity to grab her breasts and grind on her bottom. He then pulled her panties down to her ankles. He told her not to remove them.

First, he smacked her bottom with his hand, and she moaned. He then used his belt to give her the spanking that she craved. He spanked her with the belt kind of lightly, she barely moved. He then hit her bottom a little harder, and once again she barely moved. Her beautiful cushioning was protecting her well. He intentionally put more power behind his next spank, and she moaned loudly. He found her sweet spot. He would spank her slowly in different spots on her bottom until he could no longer contain himself.

He threw the belt to the floor, then told her to remove the panties. He entered her aggressively and began to pump hard and fast until he climaxed. Charlie had multiple orgasms but wanted more. She was turned all the way up, and this entire night made her higher than any amount of alcohol could ever make her. Zhon also wanted more but needed some time to regroup.

Charlie just laid on the bed with her eyes closed enjoying her euphoric state, waiting for Zhon to give her more. She was so numbed up from the endorphins that were released, that she barely felt the stings that she would feel later, from the spanking that she received. The spanking that would also leave a lasting physical memory for the rest of the week. A physical memory that she welcomed. They would have sex two more times that night, that would leave them both exhausted.

Devon.

Devon had been Charlie's assistant since the beginning. They had worked together in the past, and she knew that Devon had strong customer service skills. Something that was very important to Charlie. She wasn't going to be another Black-owned business with a bad reputation of having employees with attitudes. Charlie had been in customer service most of her career and knew the importance of being thoughtful and kind to customers. Also, knowing how to deal with needy customers and difficult customers. Devon had proven to be a gem when it came to all of that. Charlie paid her a little more than she could really afford but having patrons who wanted to keep returning because of a great atmosphere, and outstanding customer service, was going to make that up in no time, and it did.

Devon's husband would pick her up every-day, and Charlie couldn't help but notice that he didn't seem to like her. Even though he half spoke to her, he did speak, so she continued to speak to him despite his crappy responses. One day, Charlie asked Devon why her husband always seemed to have an attitude. She told Charlie, that he didn't like her being around single women because they liked to hook their married girlfriends up with other men. She said that he probably never got over his ex-wife leaving him for another man, and he blamed her (his ex-wife's) girlfriend for it. Charlie finally understood.

One day, one of Charlie's regulars, Hank, told her to keep an eye on him (Devon's husband), because he would stare at her from a table in the far corner. Charlie never noticed him doing that. She told Hank, "okay" and thanked him. He let her know that if she ever needed him, to call him, because he lived close by, so she thanked him again. She did keep that in mind and knew that his number was in the café's loyalty system.

"You know how I feel about you lady!"

He smiled at Charlie, and she smiled back. She was used to a lot of her male patrons having a little crush on her. Her friendliness was greatly appreciated and sometimes they would mistake it for something more, but she always handled it.

She wasn't sure what to make of Hank's warning. She would bring it up to her niece Tara, who ran the consignment shop next door. Tara told her that he was probably one of those men who secretly admired her, but knew that he couldn't have or handle someone like her. Charlie just laughed, but Tara assured her that those types of men existed, and not to discount that.

"Well, that wouldn't be my problem anyway, that would-be Devon's problem."

"Okay, Auntie! But if you ever need me, I'm here!"

"Okay, Sweetness! And thank you!" She gave Tara a hug and kiss, then went back next door to the café.

Homey.

One of Zhon's friends came into Parlons, looking for Charlie. She knew him from seeing him at different events, and she knew that he and Zhon were friends. He had heard about the café through word of mouth, and he had heard that Charlie was the owner. Francke had a crush on Charlie, but he had no idea that she and Zhon were as close as they were. They both maintained a lot of discretion with their relationship, and Charlie was extremely protective of it because they had a lot of mutual associates, and she didn't want any of them to know about her and Zhon. She liked the clandestineness of their friendship. The secrecy made it untouchable to the outside world for her, and she felt protective of his reputation.

Charlie embraced Francke and told him that it was nice to see him, and he felt likewise. Francke ordered a beer and some hors d'oeuvres, then asked Charlie to sit and talk with him. They would get into a discussion about the state of brick and mortar businesses.

"What you have here with Parlons is an experience. That is what all brick and mortars are going to have to provide, if they want to maintain an onsite business for people to come to."

"I agree with that, and I heard somewhere recently that retail is going to eventually be a mostly online business in the future. That really makes sense to me. With Amazon becoming damn near a monopoly in the business, who is going to be able to really compete with them. They already help you to find your items for the cheapest price. They are shipping for same day service. They are now in the food business and can deliver your groceries same day. I mean what they can do is endless as far as shopping, and if you're not working for or if you're not selling through Amazon, how can you ever compete? Especially the little guys."

"Yeah, the only way I believe the little guys will be able to compete is like I mentioned earlier; they have to create an experience in their establishment. Something that you can't get by going online to do business. Something that we crave and need as social beings. That face to face and physical contact that you will never be able to get online."

"Exactly! And that's exactly why I opened up Parlons, to get back to having real conversations with real people. Human interaction is invaluable for so many reasons. This generation of kids that are coming up, is getting ruined because of these electronics and social media. They are not learning to socialize in the real world; they are not learning conflict resolution, and they are not learning critical thinking skills.

We see this too often now with children not being able to handle conflict, to the point that they are taking their lives over things that people have had to deal with, and did in the past. It's not their fault, it's the fault of society and what we are allowing to happen to these children. Technology has advanced a whole lot faster, than our ability to adapt to it. We *have* to get these kids back to socializing, and not on social media, but in real live human environments so that they don't become socially handicapped."

"Absolutely!", said Francke.

Once that conversation finished, Francke let Charlie know that he had been digging her for some time now and wanted to know if they could go out. Charlie turned him down and let him know that she already had a couple of friends who she was seeing.

Charlie did have an attraction to Francke, but because she was close friends with Zhon, and he and Zhon were friends, that made him off limits as someone who she could be closer too.

Charlie had boundaries and limits when it came to the men that she would deal with. Anyone who was considered a friend of Zhon was off limits because she dealt with Zhon. She had made her choice within that group of friends, so no one else in that circle could ever be with her, because of Zhon. This wasn't anything that was discussed with Zhon, this was just how she kept things uncomplicated, and this was how she was raised.

It was never okay to deal with someone who was close friends with a boyfriend or girlfriend, former or otherwise. This was seen as a betrayal, and Charlie came from a family where betrayal was something that could get you ostracized, in any way that betrayal presented itself. Even though she wasn't Zhon's woman, she wouldn't feel right dealing with his friend. This was about her own moral compass, and what was instilled in her since childhood. She understood it and lived by it. Francke was a bit disappointed, but that wasn't going to stop him from trying again in the future.

Girls Night Out.

Charlie, her girlfriend Bree, and three of Bree's girlfriends decided to have a girl's night out. Bree was Charlies closest girlfriend who she loved and adored for being a down to earth, beautiful person. Bree wasn't gossipy, petty or judgmental, and she genuinely loved Charlie for her strength and realness. Charlie saw her as beautiful, classy, smart, strong, and as someone who respected her time and space, exactly what she needed in a girlfriend. She was Charlie's roadie whenever she wanted to hang out. Bree was more of a social butterfly than

Charlie, and Charlie always enjoyed spending time with her.

They would all meet up at the café, then ride in Charlie's car to go out to dinner, then to her brother's sports-bar. They always had a good time when they hung out. Bree's girlfriends were always as classy and down to earth as she was, just the type of women that Charlie enjoyed being around. They were all professional Black women, so Charlie always had pride in the crew.

There was a lawyer (Joy), a doctor (Janet), a scientist (Vera), and a CFO (Bree); and Charlie was the entrepreneur. They decided to go to a nice Japanese restaurant and hoped that they didn't need a reservation because this was a last-minute decision. They were able to get a table and decided to order things that they could eat as a group, instead of ordering separately. They wouldn't be able to take anything with them since they were going to the sports bar afterward. The ladies decided to get a couple of sushi and sashimi platters as hors d'oeuvres, and then they would order a spread of tempura, with some Japanese vegetables.

Joy began to talk about her new lover and his sexual proclivities…

"I don't mind doing it occasionally, but he wants it all the time," said Joy. "I never had a man want anal before him, and he introduced me to it. I was scared at first because I heard that it was painful, and it is, but he helped me to learn to relax and now I enjoy it; but all the time? I'm starting to wonder if he's just gay."

Janet spoke up. "That doesn't mean that he's gay, maybe he just enjoys anal sex. And what if he is gay? Are you guys in a committed relationship? Are you trying to get married? If you're just having fun, what difference does it make if two consenting adults decide to have sex? He's still a man with a penis, and if his penis wants to be inside of you, and you don't mind where it wants to go inside of you, what's the problem. And I hope that you're using condoms."

"Yes, we are using condoms, and no to the committed relationship and looking to get married question, but I'm not trying to end up with feelings and he really likes men."

"Well, why don't you ask him about it, what makes you think that he likes men, other than him liking anal sex? Does he like other parts of your body, how does he look at you, do you guys kiss?"

"He loves my body and my boobs. He likes to look at me, tells me that I have a beautiful figure, and he loves sucking on my boobs and kissing me too."

"Girl, that man aint gay! And I also say, so what if he was? You are two people enjoying each other sexually. Let me tell you something! I have a male friend who told me that he lived a gay lifestyle for years. He had been molested as a child, and it caused him a lot of confusion about his sexuality. So, he thought that he was gay, because that was the only kind of sex he had ever had, and he said that he liked it. Then he became good friends with a female, and he started having feelings for her, and she for him; and she knew that he was gay, or living a gay lifestyle.

They ended up having a relationship, and he said that the feelings and the sex that they had together, made him question his sexuality. He had never felt like that about or with anyone else before. It only lasted for 6 months, but he said that he went back to one of his former male lovers, and he just didn't feel the same about the sex with men anymore. And he said that he became a little obsessed with sex with women for a while. He began to prefer it and had to truly evaluate his sexuality from then on.

He's in therapy now for what happened to him as a kid, but he believes that he'll find out through therapy if he's really gay, or if it's because of the molestation. Look, even if he figures out that he is gay, I hope that he understands that love is love; and that sex is just a part of it.

If I met a man who was everything that I needed him to be, and I was everything that he needed me to be, then told me that he used to live a gay lifestyle, but he realized that he wasn't really gay, I would definitely give that relationship a chance. Of course, there would have to be a lot of talking and communicating before we were to undertake a relationship, but girl, finding a man that you connect with in a special way, is worth giving it a try.

The biggest factor in all of that would be to constantly communicate, be open and be honest with each other. That way if he starts to feel that he made a mistake, it would be an easier transition for you both. Some of these sick men out here have messed up a lot of men and women by raping them as children. It's a fucking shame!"

Charlie and the rest of the ladies listened intently, then Vera had a few words to say.

"Okay, we're getting carried away here! The man likes anal sex, and that's all that you are sure about. Stop speculating and ask the man, tactfully. You are a grown and educated woman; you can do that. Just ask him why he enjoys anal sex so much, and please don't play with your words; be direct without insulting the man."

"I agree, ladies," said Charlie. "It's too stressful to try figuring out why people like what they like sexually; just enjoy it. But if you're concerned about his sexual orientation, then you must address it if that's bothering you, but just know that you could insult him too, so choose your words carefully. No one likes to be judged for their fetishes. He may not even know why he likes anal sex so much. Or maybe it's new for him too, so he's riding the wave, so to speak."

Charlie giggled a bit after she said that, but she made it clear that she was serious about choosing her words carefully. Saying the wrong thing could cause hurt feelings that can't be reversed.

They all had a good time eating and conversing. Now they were on their way to the sports bar. They all smoked cigars, and lit up after Charlie put her top down, and pulled off in her black on black Cadillac convertible. The Eagles were playing that night, so the ladies were decked out in their Eagles gear. They knew how to sexy up their wardrobe, and they got plenty of attention when they walked through the doors of the establishment.

Taylin had a thing for Bree, and he would see the crew coming through the door, but he went right to Bree, grabbed her arm, and escorted her to the booth that he had held for them.

Charlie said, "Well **Damn**!!! Can we all get an escort? What's up with that?"

They all started laughing because Taylin always ignored Charlie and everyone else when Bree was around. He would hold her hand as she got comfortably in her seat after he gave her a hug and kiss on the cheek. Bree enjoyed his attention, and she never had to pay for a thing when she was there. Well, none of them did when they came with Charlie, but when Bree came without her, she still never needed to use her own money.

They all followed Bree and Taylin to the table but stayed out of the way until Taylin was finished his seating of Bree. They would always tease Bree about his attraction to her, but she just laughed and called them all haters.

They enjoyed the game, especially since the Eagles won that night. They would get up to leave and say their goodbyes to Taylin and Jerrell. The fella's walked the ladies to the car, and Taylin and Bree had a brief conversation before they hugged each other and kissed each other on the cheek.

"Would y'all go 'head with that!" Charlie couldn't resist messing with her brother and Bree about their flirting.

Taylin responded, "How about you shut up and go ahead about your business in your pimpmobile. How many hoes you got now?" Charlie just cracked up laughing, because he had no idea that she did have a few lovers, and his pimp and hoe remark tickled her as she thought about her situation. The ladies teased Bree as they pulled off, as she knew they would, and Bree called them all haters like she always did, and they all laughed.

Unfaithful

Charlie started to feel some kind of way about dealing with a married man. She would hear a couple of conversations at Parlons that made her question her actions. One conversation was a group of ladies, one of which (Jasmine) was talking about her husband cheating, and was in tears trying to understand why he needed to cheat on her. One of her girlfriends (Eileen) blamed women who had no morals, and no respect for the sanctity of marriage. Another girlfriend (Kelly) blamed him and his lack of self-control and assured her that nothing that she does can change that. A third girlfriend (Sharon) believed that all men cheated, and it's something that she would have to accept if she wanted to be married, to anyone.

Eileen would kick the conversation off… "These girls out here nowadays are nothing but whores, and they make it easy for men to cheat. It's hard to even be in a relationship because there is always some chick chasing after your man. They act like they can't find a man of their own. Then they don't have any type of decency and will go down on him and have anal sex and eat his asshole out… all kinds of perverted shit. How can any wife compete with that? We need to just find this hoe and beat her ass!"

"And then what?", asked Kelly. "Even if we do beat her ass, and she leaves him alone, do you really think that he won't go find some other female to cheat with? He knows that he's married to Jasmine. He took his vowels the same day that she did. She needs to just leave his cheating ass!"

Then Sharon jumped in… "Now why would she do that? To find a better man who doesn't cheat? Where they at? All men cheat, and if you think otherwise, you're a fool!"

"Yeah, well I don't believe that! I refuse to believe that!", said Kelly.

"Well, I believe it!", said Sharon. "And the best way to deal with a cheating ass man is to cheat too. This will balance the playing field. This way it won't hurt as much, and you won't feel like a fool. There are women who build their whole lives around their husbands, and when they find out that they've cheated, they are devastated.

I know one who tried to run her husband over, but was so distraught, it ended up being his brother. That man was in the hospital for weeks. And you can imagine the guilt she felt for hurting her brother-in-law. This is why crimes of passion happen. Even though it's usually the men who kill because of cheating, women do it too.

Just think about how some women do everything that they can to support their man. Some give up school to work and help to put their man through college. Some give up careers, to be stay at home moms to take care of their homes, full time. These women alter their lives for their men, then they cheat and some even leave once they get their degrees, or find some pretty young thing who doesn't have to raise children, and get to be sexy all the time because they don't have responsibilities except to take care of themselves.

Girl, you have children and many years invested in this man. And to think that you're going to find one who doesn't cheat is foolish. Go meet someone and get even. Better yet, George has been in love with you forever, and we all know how you feel about George. Go give that man some, and make him happy, and make yourself happy too. *Fuck* Lonnie! And his dizzy *bitch*, whoever she is."

All the girls started laughing, even Jasmine. Charlie had to laugh too, although she would never believe that all men cheated. First, she rationalized the fact that no one could possibly know such a thing because no one was with all men, all the time. But she did believe that most men cheated, based on her experiences with her own husband, knowing that her father cheated on her mother many times, and her brothers cheated on their girlfriends and wives. And also, she would hear too many stories of infidelity through the years, that gave her the belief that most men did cheat. This would be *one* of the factors that made her choose to never marry again.

Then there was another conversation between a group of men about fidelity, on a different day. One of the men (Jeff) was married and bragging about having a new girlfriend who he was going to see after he left the café. A second male (Amin), and friend of the first man condemned his actions and reminded him that his wife was a good woman, who was the type of woman that any man would love to be with. Another male friend (Vance) was a lifelong bachelor who couldn't see himself ever marrying. The last friend (Steve) had a broader understanding of it all and had a solution to infidelity.

Amin was sick of Jeff's infidelities, "Jeff, you have a beautiful wife who is a good woman. How would you feel if she was cheating on you like you're cheating on her? Remember that women are better cheaters than us, man. They're smarter than us, and our ignorant asses can't even imagine the good one's cheating. That gives them the upper hand in this game, man."

"Man, I know that she's a good woman, but marriage can get a bit boring after many years with the same woman. We only live once and I'm not going to be on my death bed talking about what I wish I had done. I'd rather have regrets about what I did do."

"Man, you sound *dumb*! Who says that kind of shit!" Amin said with impatience.

Vance chimed in, "I get what he's saying, but I'd rather just stay single than to hurt a woman by cheating on her. I'll never forget being a little boy and hearing my mom crying because she found out that my dad was cheating on her. I didn't really understand what that meant then, but I somehow understood that another woman was involved, and all I could think about was getting old enough to fuck my dad up for making my mom cry.

I never forgot that feeling, and even though I love my dad, my mom's is my heart. So, when I got old enough, I told him that if I ever heard my mom cry again because of some female he was cheating with, we were going to have to have a talk. Now, I don't know if he ever cheated again after that, or if he was just more careful, but I never heard of him with another woman again.

You have to realize that people in the past and in other cultures got married for reasons other than love. They married for political alliances, or to gain wealth, and men also married women to protect and take care of them, when women weren't allowed to work and make a living. We have to remember that. Men have even married women to keep other men from being able to claim them.

In some cultures, males and females were promised to other families in arranged marriages. It didn't matter whether they liked each other or not when they finally met. Many times, these people would learn to like or love each other. Marrying for love is a more modern-day freedom for getting married, and it hasn't proven to be the best reason. Even now, love has proven to be the least likely factor to determine a long-term marriage.

For me, I know that I can't stay faithful, and I wouldn't want to cheat on any woman, because I witnessed the pain of infidelity through my mother. I love women, and I can't see myself with one woman for a lifetime. Even now that I'm older, I still can't see myself committing to one woman, so I'll just maintain my life as a bachelor. My women know what I'm about, so they know what to expect. I don't lie to them, and I'm always upfront about my shit. Many have left me alone because they knew that they couldn't handle it, and many have stayed because they could"

"Man, you're just a *hoe*! Keep it up and your dick is gonna fall off! Then you'll be useless to all of those women." Amin had to let Vance have it, and they all started laughing.

Steve had a few words to say too, "Look, by nature, men are not monogamous creatures anyhow. Monogamy is a part of our socialization. We have a primal desire to be with many women throughout our lives. Staying monogamous is a choice. Some of these religions make it seem as if it's some God-ordained law to only be with one woman. Then, many of us rationalize it as some kind of right-of-passage for being a man, to have other women. Then you have the men who have to fight temptation, with many of them believing that having desires for other women is a sin.

It's fucking crazy! But the bottom line is that fidelity is a choice. People need to get a more historical understanding of our primal state of being. They will then be able to understand why their temptations for other women are natural, and then they will be better prepared to deal with those temptations. If men were to help each other with learning to curb their behavior, instead of egging them on to be with other women, it could become a social norm to fight infidelity, than to give into it.

As couples, this needs to be a conversation before committing to each other. How and why do people commit to each other, without talking about such an important factor in marriage and divorce? Infidelity and money, and the behaviors behind these two things, which are the major causes of divorce, should be discussed before committing to each other.

People get caught up in their feelings of infatuation, love, and sex, instead of the more important understanding of each other's habits and *true* beliefs. Not the ones that you pretend to have because you know that you'll probably lose her or him; because women are catching up to men with all this bullshit now; if you are honest about those things.

Too many people are pretending in order to get what they desire, instead of being real in order to find a way to work through these things before they become a problem. People need to have deeper conversations about these things so that they can better prepare for dealing with them as a unit.

When you're young, you don't usually have the experience to even know how you might handle these situations, so that's more understandable, but these conversations should still happen then too. Now when you're older, and you're on your 10th relationship, and 2nd marriage, there should be no excuse."

The men nodded while in a daze of thought, but none of the conversations changed Jeff's mind. He still went to see his girlfriend once they parted from the café.

Having heard these two conversations in the course of one week had Charlie deep in thought. She would put Lowell on the back burner for a while until she could figure things out. She didn't quit him or anything, she just didn't make time for him.

Charlie would usually change her plans when Lowell was in town, just to make time for him. But while she was trying to understand why she dealt with married men, (even though she was cheated on as a wife), she just didn't change her plans to be with him like she usually did.

The Decision.

Charlie had to do a lot of soul-searching and reflecting to try to understand her lack of concern whether a man who she wanted to deal with was married or not. She understood that American society frowned on infidelity because it broke the religious vows that were committed to, in the name of God and religion. It also broke the legal contract of the marriage bond. She didn't have much tolerance for religion, nor did she respect the legal system for how it handled the marriage contract. Many lawyers would take advantage of the emotions that the action of divorce would evoke, by instigating issues to make more money.

Ever since she realized that societal norms and moralities didn't represent or protect her, and she decided to live her life on her own terms, she could no longer just follow some rules that were expected of the "good girl" that she grew up being, and that she did try to follow. Those rules didn't work out for her, nor could they ever make her happy. She realized that her happiness was in her hands, and her hands alone.

Charlie had gone through a dark period in her life, where she questioned life itself and didn't know if she had the strength or courage to live another day. Once she got through her dark period, she decided that she was going to do whatever she desired to do, despite what anyone else would think of those things. She knew that she needed to be discreet because of societies judgments, although she told herself that she would never do anything that she would be ashamed of if her actions were revealed in some way; whether it would be someone trying to hurt her, or someone running their mouths for some reason. No one would ever be able to blackmail her because she wouldn't be ashamed of anything that she chose to do to enjoy her life and to keep herself happy. And if there were any consequences to any of her actions, she would accept full responsibility for them.

So, some of her rules were to allow herself to connect with people, things, and situations that pleased her, and added positivity and joy to her life's experience. If she met someone, and she had an attraction to them and enjoyed spending time with them beyond the ordinary, that person became special to her. Now the extent of special depended on their connection. It could be someone that she enjoyed conversing with, or someone she liked hanging out with, or someone who she had a strong sexual attraction to.

Her lack of wanting or needing to ask questions of people was a personality fault in this instance. So, she usually didn't ask personal questions when she met people because she never intentionally set out to meet friends or lovers. This is something that would occur, based on time spent with someone, so by the time she felt a strong attraction, finding out he was married wasn't a strong enough deterrent. This was her realization of her reasons for being with a married man. So, going forward, she would make sure that she found out if a man was married before she even became friendly with him. This would help to deter her future actions, but it couldn't change the events of the past.

Bree.

Charlie hadn't seen Bree in months, and when she stepped through the doors of Parlons, she was happy and excited to see her. Bree always understood Charlies need for space and would forever respect that. So, she would check on her whenever too many months went by without hearing from her, even though that was normal behavior for Charlie. They grabbed each other hugged, rocked back and forth, and kissed each other firmly on the cheek. They asked how each other was doing and how their families were doing, and everyone was well. They got all the preliminaries out of the way, so now they can get their rap on and catch up with each other, they couldn't wait. Charlie still had Lowell on her mind and the dilemma of being with a married man. So, she would discuss this with Bree…

"So, what's been going on with you lady?", asked Bree.

"Well…"

Charlie explained about the two conversations, and about her feelings about dealing with a married man. She explained to Bree that even though she had come to terms with that in the past, she had been thinking deeply, trying to understand how she, being a woman who had been cheated on by her husband, could be involved in the same activity.

"But Charlie, don't you ever want to be in a committed relationship with someone? You deserve to have the best because you are such a genuinely nice and a good person."

"Bree, it's just not important to me. I've been married before and I've been in love after that. I'm just not interested in going from relationship to relationship to find that person who loves me the way that I deserve to be loved, and who I love in the same way. You know that I've attempted a couple of relationships, but my tolerance for bullshit is really low. Also, I just haven't met anyone who I miss that much, where I would want them in my space on a daily basis."

"But you don't have to be with anyone on a daily basis to be in a committed relationship with them. It's just nice to have someone to feel love for, and to cuddle with, and to just sit and do nothing with. And it's nice to have someone to be there for you when you need another person, for just anything. *And* it's nice to have someone to have sex with regularly."

"Now I have to say Amen to that because it would certainly be nice to have sex more often, but that's not enough to make me want to be in a relationship. I love my freedom. I don't have to deal with the jealousy of someone getting upset at my customers for having a crush on me. Or thinking that every man who I deal with as a business associate somehow wants me. And if for some fantastic reason that it was true, would they trust me to handle it. Man, I don't feel like dealing with any of that."

"Charlie, every man isn't your ex-husband!"

"I do realize that, but I've seen that same behavior in many. And I would honestly love to meet a man who could change my mind about the way that I feel, but that doesn't happen. I'm content with being single, and I'm happy. What can rival happy?"

"Okay, so let's talk about your dilemma and the fact that you are questioning your choice to deal with a married man, what's that about? If it's an issue, then why don't you just deal with someone who isn't married?" Charlie laughed.

"It's not that simple. I can't make myself like someone just because they aren't married. I can't just dislike someone just because they are. Who I like is something that happens because we have a unique connection, I don't seek that out and I don't get that with too many people. And when I meet a guy who's single that I really like, once enough times passes, I begin to understand why they are single. Too many people have too many issues out here. There are a lot of damaged and broken people walking around who need therapy, but they either don't see it, or they are in denial. I don't have the time, patience, or desire to attempt to fix anyone. I have my own shit that I'm constantly evaluating so that I'm not bringing that kind of madness to anyone."

"What about the wife? You've been there before, and you were a wife who was cheated on. How can you involve yourself in doing the same thing? Remember Charlie, I'm not judging you. I'm just trying to help you think through your dilemma."

"I know babe, and I don't feel judged by you. I appreciate you helping me to think through this. To answer your question, when I was the wife being cheated on, I never blamed the women. I blamed the man who made a commitment to me. He was the one betraying me. Those women had nothing to do with my relationship with him. Why blame them, when even if I were able to convince them to stay away from him, he would just find other women to cheat with.

This issue was his, and he was the one who needed to reconcile his choice to break our commitment, by cheating with other women. I reconciled my choice to stay with him through this betrayal, by divorcing his ass. He has remarried, and he's doing the same thing with his second wife. Like I said, the issue was his.

To bring this back to Lowell, I don't know why he chooses to cheat on his wife, and I don't want to know, it's none of my business. Even if I did want to know, I'm only gonna get his side of the story, and there are two sides to it."

"Then there's the truth," said Bree.

"No disrespect Bree, but I hate the saying that 'There's his side, there's her side, then there's the truth,' because that isn't accurate unless they are both just lying. There's only his perception of the truth and her perception of the truth. There is no objective truth about what each of them believes to be the truth. No one else is a part of their relationship or in their heads to verify what they believe the truth to be. Even having a mediator to help them through their issues would only give them someone who can help them to see each other's perception of their issues. No one knows every detail that led to their issues, and even then, they are perceptions of what's true. Only he knows why he's doing what he's doing, and only she knows what she thinks, feels, and believes about that. No one else can possibly know an objective truth about their issues."

Bree just sat back and listened.

"And to get back to what I was saying, all men who cheat aren't bad men, and I can't dislike men because they do such a thing because, in my experiences and understandings, most men do it. And all men don't do it for the same reasons. One of the guys during the conversations that I mentioned, said that fidelity is a choice, and I agree with that. He also mentioned how men aren't monogamous by nature, and I have heard that before, and it makes sense to me. Although I don't like the thought of being the person who is a part of that betrayal, I can't dislike the man for his behavior. Also, there are women who accept infidelity as an eventual part of marriage. This is the more unlikely scenario, but I choose not to be a part of figuring that out."

"Okay, so what if his wife finds out and approaches you, what then?"

"Well, it depends on how she approaches me, so I can't really answer that question. But I can tell you how I feel about that happening. First, if his wife approaches me, then that will end the relationship because I feel like any man who decides to involve himself with a woman outside of his marriage, needs to know how to handle his shit. She should also realize that I'm not her problem. I'm not that special... at least not in the realm of their relationship. She will win if she approaches me because I understand that she is the most important person in this trio. Me leaving him alone does not fix the issue that's causing him to decide to cheat, but she wins."

This was a much-needed conversation for Charlie, but she still needed time to figure things out.

Accepting the Burden.

So, Charlie needed to decide what she was going to do about Lowell. She had a talk with him, to let him know that she was having some feelings about dealing with him being married, and although it wasn't an issue in the past, she wanted to make some positive changes in her life. He told her that he understood. A few months had passed, and Lowell would call her about once a month to check on her. She did think about him and definitely felt a void in her life, but as long as he kept his distance, she was good.

One night, Lowell called her when she was lying in bed thinking, and he happened to be on her mind. She was happy to hear from him, and he was missing her and saying all the things that she didn't need to hear him say; he was pulling her back in.

Even though Charlie ended it, she couldn't come up with a good reason anymore, to stay away from a man whom she adored, and who adored her. A man who she wasn't trying to make her own, nor would she allow that to happen. A man who would probably find a new lover in time, if he didn't already have another one. A man whose infidelities weren't because of her, but were an end to a means for him. They had made a connection that couldn't be erased. The damage was done, and that couldn't be changed. These were the thoughts that rationalized her decision to continue their sexual relationship. She accepted the burden of her conscience and any consequences that resulted from her decision. Lowell was on his way to "fuck" her, and she couldn't wait to be "fucked" by him.

Stalker

Charlie was done for the day. She went to the parking garage to get into her car to go home, and she saw a note on her windshield. It was on white paper, folded in half, and stuck under her wiper blade. She pulled it out, opened it, then read it…

"Bitch, watch your back!"

She looked around wondering who could have or would have put this on her windshield, and why? "Maybe they had the wrong car", she thought. She didn't let it bother her too much, but she didn't want anyone harming her car thinking that it was someone else's. There were no live attendants there, so she made a mental note to contact the parking lot company the next day, to see if they had any cameras on her car, and to alert them of the note.

By the next day, she had forgotten all about it, and went into work without even thinking about the parking lot company. A few days went by, and one morning when she went to Parlons to open up, there were a bunch of dead flowers laying in front of her door. She just looked down at them for a few seconds with a confused frown on her face. When she picked them up, there was a note attached to them.

"You fucking slut, these are the only kind of flowers you deserve!"

Now she knew that the other note wasn't a mistake. This note and the dead flowers were intentional, and she knew that they were meant for her; she just had no clue who would leave her such mean notes, and dead flowers.

When Devon came into work, she showed her the note, and told her about the note that was left on her car. She told Charlie to call the cops, but Charlie wasn't interested in doing that. Her instincts told her not to alert the police, just in case she had to have something done to the culprit that might end in physical harm, or worse. This was how things were handled in her family growing up. If it were a business incident, she would keep everything above board and handle it by the book; but this was personal, and instead of instilling fear in her, it put her in fight mode.

She would talk to her two brothers that day and tell them what was going on, and Jerrell told her if anything else happened, to let him and Taylin know. A week went by, and Charlie noticed someone driving behind her for almost her entire 20-minute ride home. She pulled off the road into a parking space to let them pass by her before she would continue her ride home. They turned off before they got to her, so she couldn't see who it may have been. She just noticed that they had a front license plate on a black car, and that it was from New Jersey.

She called her brothers that night to let them know that she believed someone had followed her that night. Jerrell told her that they would take care of it. Charlie didn't know exactly what her brothers were going to do, but she knew that if they said they would handle it, they would.

Jerrell and Taylin were from the streets, and even though they owned a sports bar together, they still stayed connected to them. They used their hustle money to buy into a legitimate business to get away from the dead-end lifestyle of the streets. They still used street tactics to handle many of their issues, and they kept their boys that they grew up with, close. They all played different roles in their business, and they also handled a lot of their issues by way of hood justice.

Her brothers would send some of their boys to take turns, two at a time, to watch Charlies car for a few hours at a time. They would have their boys rotate in three-hour shifts, while she was at work, then they would follow her home every night. They would stay far enough behind her to allow anyone who was going to follow her, to do so; but they stayed close enough to keep her in their sight. They would watch her car and follow her home every-day for two weeks, but nothing happened, so her brothers pulled their boys off of their detail.

Taylin would tell Charlie to go get herself a gun, specifically a Glock 19 compact, and to start target practice. He would also tell her to get her license to carry. She did what her brother told her to do, but she didn't wait to receive her license to start carrying her gun. She wasn't unfamiliar with handling a gun, but she hadn't wanted to use or carry one in years. At this point, she felt threatened by the recent events, and she wasn't about to become anyone's victim, without preparing to protect herself and fight back.

She kept trying to figure out who would dislike her so much to leave such hateful notes, and to try to frighten her. She was certain that it wasn't anyone who knew her well, because they would know what kind of backup she had, and they would know that she didn't do fear. An attempt to frighten her would put her in defense mode, and it would also piss her off to no end. But Charlie didn't allow anger to cloud her reasoning. It pushed her into a calm that allowed her to assess everything around her and to prepare for as many potential incidents that she could think of. Mostly in her head, but she moved and prepared on the side of caution, with her daily routines.

She got the feeling that it was more likely a man, because they didn't harm her car, and they left flowers, although they were dead ones; but who? She thought about Joey, and New York, and even Devon's husband, but she still couldn't imagine any of them being that deeply hateful toward her. She wasn't so naïve as to completely rule anyone out, but she attempted to get a more focused perspective on who it could possibly be, so that she could rule out the more obvious. She would then pay attention to the less obvious, until she figured out who it was.

There were no more incidents for the next few weeks, so she wasn't sure if the person was close enough around her to see or hear some things to alert them, or if they had a change of heart about what they were doing to her. Charlie preferred this thing play itself out, so that she wouldn't be suspicious of everyone around her, but she couldn't allow it to cause her to be paranoid, so she didn't. She would relax about it, but be cautiously aware of it all. She would carry her gun every-day, and she would keep the brass knuckles that Taylin gave her, in her back pocket.

The Incident.

A few more weeks would go by with no issues, then one night when Charlie was on her way home, someone seemed to be following her again. So, she pulled off the street into a parking space again, but it was sooner than she had before, and once again, the car turned before it got to her. This time it was a different car, it was gray with no front license plate. She called Jerrell to let him know what was going on. He told her to just go home, and he would have someone sit outside of her building for the night.

Jerrell would make sure that she would be followed every night once she got off. One night they noticed a car following her for almost the length of her ride home. Charlie noticed it too, but also knew that she was being protected. The two guys that her brother put on her, got in front of the car, with their car, and jumped out. They were strapped with their guns exposed, when each one stepped on each side of the car and told the driver to turn both front windows down, or they were going to break them. He nervously rolled his windows down and asked what was wrong.

"Unlock the door!" Zoe, her brother's boy, wanted the guy out of the car.

"What did I do, man?"

Zoe pulled his gun out.

"Unlock the mutha fuckin door, or I'll blow the lock off, with you behind it!"

The guy unlocked the door but was obviously terrified.

"Now get the fuck out the car!"

He hesitantly got out, and Zoe returned his gun to his holster, then grabbed the guy by his neck and slammed him against the car. Haney was still on the other side of the car keeping an eye out.

"Why the fuck, were you following Charlie?", Zoe asked loudly.

"*What*!?!"

Zoe pulled him by his neck and his shirt, then slammed him back on the car.

"Don't fuckin play with me! Why the fuck, were you following the lady?"

"Mannn, I wasn't following anybody! I'm on my way to the store!"

By that time, Charlie came back around to see who was following her, and it was Devon's husband. She stared in confusion for a minute while Zoe was still interrogating him and bouncing him against the car. She wasn't sure if he was telling the truth, but she could see the fear in his eyes, and she didn't want to do anything to hurt Devon, so she pulled Zoe to the side and told him to let him go, and why. They both could tell that if he were the culprit, that he would unlikely pull such a stunt again.

Devon would call Charlie that night and explain to her that her husband was indeed going to a shopping center near where she lived. The store that he needed to go to, was the only one in the area. Charlie chose to believe her and apologized for his treatment. If this were true, then they still didn't catch the person who was trying to scare her. She relayed the information to her brothers, so they would continue to send the boys to keep an eye on her as she traveled home every night.

Two weeks would pass again with no incident, so her brothers pulled their boys off watching her again, and told her to keep her gun on her every day, and to continue with her target practice and defensive training. They also told her to be cautious and to pay attention to her instincts about every and anyone. Charlie did as her brothers told her.

One day, Hank, one of her regular patrons, had drank a few too many beers and had gotten chatty with Charlie. She knew not to serve him anymore and had given Devon the signal not to serve him anymore beer. While talking with Charlie, he would ask her why she never called him or went out with him. Charlie told him that she already had a couple of friends and that she had no time or space for anymore. Hank would try to sell her on how much better he would treat her than anyone else, but Charlie just smiled and said,

"I'm sure that you would, Hank, but I'm not looking for any new friends."
Hank would change the subject and talk about his work at a car dealership in New Jersey. And would go on about how his co-workers would steal his customers. Charlie had known Hank for almost a year, and his behavior was odd to her, but she understood that everyone went through stressful times. He would bend her ear for a few minutes more, then he decided to leave.

Charlie was a bit relieved, because she didn't want to have to refuse him drinks, but he seemed to be aware of his own limits.

At the end of her workday, Charlie went to get into her car, and there was another note under her wiper blade.

"I'm going to fuck the shit out of you, bitch, no matter how many boyfriends you have."

Her thoughts went right to the conversation that she had with Hank. She tried to remember who else was in the Café during that conversation, and she wasn't sure how many people could have heard it. She went back to the Café to review her security tapes to try to see who could have possibly overheard the conversation, and perhaps be the one to write the note. She informed her brothers about what was going on, and Jerrell told her to keep them updated.

She wrote down all the names of the patrons that she knew was in the shop when Hank was talking to her. She tried to rule out those who she knew couldn't have written that note. There were a few people in there that she never saw before, but didn't really think they were involved in the writing of the note.

Charlie racked her brain enough trying to figure out who wrote the note, then decided to just go home for the day. Once again, someone seemed to be following her, with a New Jersey front plate on the car again, but this time it was a white car. Charlie thought about the fact that Hank said that he worked at a dealership in New Jersey, and that he was the one who she told about her having a couple of friends, but she didn't want to believe that he was the culprit. She never got that kind of vibe from him. He liked her, sure, but to threaten her and call her such vile names wasn't like him at all.

She wasn't sure at all that it was Hank, but she did her usual and pulled off the road into a parking space, and as usual the car that was following her turned before passing her. So, instead of going home, she knew where Hank lived, so she would go back to the Café and walk back to the street that he lived on to see if the car was near his address. She didn't see it, but as she was walking back to the shop, the car had turned the corner. She hid behind a building until she could see who got out of the car. It was Hank! He seemed like he was still a bit inebriated, as he walked to his home and went in the door. She called her brothers and told them what happened, and she gave them Hanks address as they requested. They told her to go home and that they would handle it.

She was really disappointed in Hank, but she was also very angry that he would do such cowardice things like call her names in a note, threaten her, and follow her, while attempting to get her to go out with him. His passive aggressive behavior had her wondering what kind of psychopath he really was.

Vince.

Charlie's ex-husband was with her brothers when she called them to let them know what she discovered about Hank. He was furious when Taylin filled him in on what was going on and told them to let him handle it. He was still in love with Charlie, but Charlie wanted no parts of him. That didn't stop him from caring about her and being protective of her. She was his first wife, and even though he wasn't a good husband to her, he loved her more than any woman that he would meet after her. Time, maturity, and other women would make him aware of just how much he messed up by not appreciating her when he had her. This would be a small chance at a bit of redemption for him, and this was right up his alley, so her brothers allowed him to lead the events that would follow.

Vince got his crew together and went to Hanks home in the middle of the night. It would be six of them, all in black with ski masks on. They were prepared to break into his home with quiet skill, but Hank didn't lock his front door. And he was asleep on his sofa.

Vince told one of his boys to wake him up, and he did. Hank didn't know what was going on, but he thought that he was about to die, being surrounded by six men in black with ski masks on. Vince pulled his ski mask off, because he wanted Hank to know exactly who he was, and why he was there. He stepped toe to toe and face to face with Hank.

"So, you got a thing for Charlie, huh?"

Hank was confused at first, then things slowly began to make sense to him, but how did they know, and who were they? He didn't say a thing.

"Are you deaf? Why the fuck were you stalking Charlie and writing her fucked up notes?"

Hank still wouldn't talk, so Vince right hooked his jaw. Hanks body and head jerked to the left of Vince, then when he was able to get his bearings, he took a boxing stance. This made Vince quite happy, because now he could "fuck him up" fair and square. He used to box and could have turned pro, but didn't. But he always kept his skill sharp and enjoyed using his hands to settle altercations. He told his boys to step back so that they could get it on. Vince punched Hank in the face again, so this started a brawl between them. Hank would be a willing opponent, but was no match for Vince.

Vince let Hank get a few jabs at him, but then he used every bit of his skill, throwing a flurry of punches to incapacitate Hank, then beat him into a bloody unconsciousness. He told four of his boys to wait outside in the cars. He kept his right-hand man with him. Vince waited until Hank regained consciousness, then told him that if he ever went near Charlie again, he would kill him, and no one would ever find his body.

Resolved.

Charlies brothers would call her in the morning and let her know that the stalker situation was resolved. They also reluctantly told her that her ex-husband handled it, and Charlie was furious.

"Why the fuck would y'all let that crazy mutha fucka handle my shit? You know that I don't want any parts of that man in any of my business."

Taylin tried to convince her that he was the best person to do the job, "Yeah, well he was here when you called and wanted to handle it. Who better to handle a situation like this than V?"

"I thought that y'all were going to take care of it.!"

"We did!", said Taylin.

"Is he still…" Jerrell knew what she wanted to ask, but knew not to use certain words over the phone.

"Yes, he is…" Charlie breathed a sigh of relief. Even though she was upset at her brothers for allowing her ex to handle it, she was grateful that it was handled, and told them so.

While Charlie was at work at the café, she heard some of the regular patrons buzzing about how Hank was beaten almost to death, and how he was put into a medically induced coma, so that the swelling in his brain could go down. Charlie felt a pang of sorrow, then quickly reminded herself of the reason that he was put in that condition. This was the way that she chose to handle it, and knew that death could be the ending result of responding to threats on her own well-being. He had to be stopped before he hurt her, and he had to pay for his actions. He brought this on himself.

As the conversations about Hank continued throughout the day, she found out that he was a paranoid schizophrenic, and that his mother had died recently, and he was extremely close to her. In response, he stopped taking his medication about the same time that Charlie started getting the notes and being followed. Everything began to make sense to Charlie, but she couldn't allow herself to feel any regret, so she kept reminding herself as to why this all happened, and she continued to keep her own well-being at the top of her mind, as the reason for all of this; her conscience was clear.

Charlie would never see Hank again, but she would hear that he had healed physically, but had a scar on his face from the beating. He also got back on his medication, and had his brother staying with him to try to help keep him on track. Eventually, she wouldn't hear any talk of Hank again, and she was good with that.

I Miss You, Charlie!

New York walked through the doors of the café, scanning the shop for Charlie. He didn't see her but still decided to sit down and place an order with a new girl who worked there. As Charlie returned from running out to get supplies needed for the upcoming weekend, she entered from the rear; so, New York didn't know that she was there.

So, as his last piece of sweet potato pie sits on his plate, a pie that he usually devoured quickly, he checks his watch. He notices that it's been almost thirty minutes, and he decides not to wait any longer. He grabs his fork, scoops up the last piece of the pie, and finishes it. He then grabs his coffee and swallows what's left of it. He gets up then walks to the counter to pay. The new girl waits on him…

"How was everything?"

"Great as usual," he replies. "What is your name, by the way?"

"Mary!"

"Nice to meet you, Mary! You're new here."

"Yes, I started two weeks ago."

"Cool! Good luck with your new job!"

"Thank you!" Mary smiled as she made eye contact with New York. They exchange money, and as she hands him his change, he cracks a slight grin.

"Thank you," she says as she gently places the change in his hand. "Come again!"

"Thank You!" New York replies.

As he turns to walk out, Mary, who was clearly attracted to him, watches as he walks through the glass doors, until he was no longer in her sight. Charlie walks in, just as he steps out of sight.

"How was everything while I was gone?"

"Pretty quiet," Mary replied.

Charlie began restocking supplies, and had her back to the door and café, as New York walked back in. Mary's eyes lit up, thinking that he had an attraction to her, and returned to get her number. As he approached the counter, Mary smiled and asked,

"Did you forget something?"

He had forgotten that he wanted to buy a couple slices of pie to take with him, as he normally did. Eating them while at home, was a subtle reminder of Charlie. He saw Charlie behind the counter stocking things up, and his heart and face lit up. He didn't say a word and just stood at the counter, with his finger to his lips, waiting for Charlie to turn around.

Charlie, always listening, became curious about the awkward silence. She turned around to see what was happening. She saw New York and froze for a few seconds, then smiled because she was happy to see him.

"Hello, Charlie!"

"Hey, New York!"

"How have you been?"

"I'm good, and you?"

"I'm good too! Can we talk?"

Charlie came from behind the counter. She and New York hugged each other, then Charlie led the way to a corner table so that they could talk in private. She asked Mary to bring them some drinks. New York started the conversation.

"Charlie, I miss you so fucking much!"

Charlie didn't know what to say. She looked him in his eyes and began to tear up from the look on his face, and the sound of sincerity in his voice.

"I want to see you again, Charlie!"

She thinks about their last interaction at the café and hesitates to respond. New York notices that she's deep in thought, and quickly interrupts.

"I want to fuck the shit out of you again!"

Her body tenses as she looks down and closes her eyes, remembering their last sexual encounter. Charlie loved his nasty proclamation, and it turned her on, greatly. She had gotten over his childish display of the use of the word "bitch" and believed that he had learned his lesson. She would have a talk with him to make sure that it wouldn't happen again, but after she received the sex that he wanted to give her.

Mary comes over with some drinks for the two and took her time walking away, trying to be nosy about what was going on between them. Charlie started to respond to New York but didn't want Mary to overhear their conversation, so she thanked her for the drinks, then waited until she was out of listening range.

"Meet me at my place, tonight around 9."

"I'll see you then," New York responded.

New York forgot all about the pie slices that he actually came back for, but the anticipation of having sex with Charlie again would zap his appetite anyhow. As Charlie went back to restocking her shelves, Mary asked,

"So, he's a good friend of yours, huh?"

Charlie turned around and looked Mary in the eyes, as to let her know that she was asking questions that were none of her business, but she answered her question to make things clear.

"Yes, he is a good friend of mine!" Charlie maintained eye contact to allow her to get whatever curiosities she had, off of her chest. But Mary seemed to be finished with her questions, as she broke from the intense eye contact that Charlie had with her. She realized that she had misread New York's courtesies.

New York showed up on time, and Charlie couldn't wait to feel him inside of her again. She waited for him to come up to her condo and left the door open. She had on a fishnet bodysuit that she purchased that day, just for him, with heels on just how he liked her. All her parts were showing through the bodysuit. As he walked through the door, they made eye contact, then his eyes dropped as he visually ingested her in her perfect attire. She stood there long enough to let him see her from the front, then turned around and walked to her bedroom so that he could see her booty bounce with each step.

New York got lightheaded, as the blood from his head, seemed to rush to his penis, as he fumbled to lock her condo door. He couldn't wait to get back to the bedroom, as is erection seemed to lead him to where Charlie laid back on the bed, with her legs open, waiting for him to enter her. He closed the bedroom door, then walked over to her. He would lean into Charlie, and slowly bring his lips to her lips, then gently kissed her several times, face to face.

As he got to his third peck on the lips, he ran his hand through the top of her straight mohawk. He continued until he got to the back, and was able to grasp enough hair, to pull her head back and kiss her deeply. She rubbed his erection through his pants and massaged it until she felt as if it needed to be released from its confinement. She then unzipped his pants to expose his beautiful, stiff, extremely large member.

Charlie had missed looking at and kissing on, what she considered, a beautiful work of natural art. New York let go of her hair, to allow her to look at and kiss his erect penis. Charlie couldn't wait to feel it in her mouth again, as its girth spread it wide, and its length found its way to the back of her throat. New York allowed her to slowly get acquainted with his member again, as she slowly allowed it to leave her mouth, while the head of it stopped at her pursed lips, then slid to the back of her throat, again. She would do this a few times until New York needed to put it inside of another orifice.

He removed his clothes and threw them on the floor, then grabbed her hand to pull her up as he kissed her, and smacked her booty hard, three times in succession. He knew that it would turn her own, as she moaned from the spanking. He walked her over to the doorway of her bedroom, bent her over in the doorway, as she braced the wall with her hands above her head, while he leaned back on the wall behind him.

He then pulled himself out of his boxer briefs, and slowly pushed himself inside of her booty, through the crotch-hole opening in her bodysuit. He entered her anus slowly, as she moaned while allowing him to fulfill a desire that she denied him in the past. She was in the mood for his nasty antics, and he surely provided her with what they both wanted.

He would enter her with a slow steady force, as she would bear down to allow him to press himself past her sphincter. Once he passed her muscle, she sighed, then told him to "fuck her hard and fast." He would take his time inside of her, and this would cause her discomfort, and drive her crazy.

"Baby, I need you to fuck me hard and fast. That's the only way that I can handle anal sex."

New York's penis grew from her words, and she could feel every bit of it, as she moaned and pushed back on it for him to begin to thrust her the way that she needed him to. His penis was already deep inside of her, so he grabbed her hips, while her hands were against the wall in front of her, and he thrust himself inside of her, as she shoved her bottom at the same time. She screamed from the painful pleasure that she was experiencing. He would pull her from the wall while he was still inside of her, walked her to the bed, and bent her over the side of the bed; so that he could spread her booty to watch as his penis was going in and out, deep inside of her sweet anus while he enjoyed her, ravenously.

He couldn't get enough of Charlie's booty, but he couldn't pull himself out of her to prevent the intense orgasm that his member so badly needed from its thirst for Charlie through her bottom. His orgasm left him weak, as he laid on her bed, and left her anus soaked with semen. She had to go to the restroom to clean herself up before she could lay on her bed to enjoy the aftermath of that much needed nasty sex that he gave to her and himself.

They relaxed without a word for about 30 minutes. New York went into the bathroom to clean himself off. He then pulled Charlie off the bed and had her bend over the side of the bed, at the base of the bed. He put his penis inside of her vagina and began to pump her hard. He would then pull it out, walk to the base of the bed where her head was, then put himself inside her mouth. He would grab her head to sturdy it so that she could suck him off, while still bending over the side of the bed. He then removed himself from her mouth, grabbed her arm, then pushed her to her knees on the floor.

He would hold his penis until she opened her mouth for him to put it in her. He would then grab the back of her head with both hands, then thrust himself in her mouth and into her throat, as she gagged from the thrusts that he used to get as deep into her throat as she could. He knew that her hands were free to stop him whenever she wanted, but she didn't. This was her own personal challenge to accommodate every nasty, freaky, thing that he wanted to do to her. It turned her on greatly, to handle all his dirty desires.

He was at the point of climax, when he told her that he was about to come, so she grabbed his bottom so that he couldn't pull out of her mouth, and so she could swallow every drop of his semen. He would scream from the intense orgasm that followed their nasty sex-play. "Got *damn* Charlie! That shit has got me weak as all hell! *sheesh*!!! You're a fucking beast, woman."

New York went over to the bed and just flopped on it. Charlie went to grab a couple of waters for herself and New York and drank some water to chase the semen that she swallowed. She laid on the bed next to him, and they both fell asleep.

The Hiatus

Charlie had noticed that she was becoming a bit emotionally sensitive. She wasn't sure exactly what was going on, but it had been going on for a couple of months, and it seemed to be getting worse. She thought that maybe she was going through menopause, or maybe she was just at that time in her life where she needed more from the opposite sex, and it was affecting her this way, or maybe even something that she wasn't aware of. She knew this day would come when her emotions would creep up on her.

This was definitely going to affect her sex life because she knew that she couldn't continue to live her lifestyle and be emotional too; that just wouldn't work. She felt as if she were losing her ability to compartmentalize the two. She needed to step back for a while, until she could figure out what was going on with her, being in such an emotionally exposed state.

She had also noticed that she had been seeing a lot of positive articles on the positive aspects of being in a relationship. With each article that she read, she was feeling more positive about the idea of being in a relationship and felt perhaps it was time for her to think about it for herself.

This was different for Charlie because she was used to understanding her own life's experiences and perceptions as seeing most people in relationships as unhappy. She wasn't someone who believed in a bunch of hokey "it's a sign that you need to pay attention to" verbalisms, but she was a spiritual person, and she thought that it was all somehow related.

Charlie hadn't been interested in being in a relationship for many years, but she never ruled it out, and she hadn't met anyone who she would want to commit to.

But with her being in such an emotional state, and thinking that maybe it was time to consider being in a relationship, she had to decide how she was going to handle her lovers. Would she have to leave them all alone, or was she going to be able to keep one..., she just wasn't sure of what to do, and this wasn't like Charlie at all. She always understood her need for sex, and how she appreciated her lovers as men who she was sincerely attracted to, and how those attractions weren't too easy to come by.

She was certainly confused, but she let each of her lovers know that she was going through some emotional confusion, and needed to end their sexual relationships. She thought that doing this would help to give her some clarity, and she knew that none of her lovers were going to be valid choices to take that next step with. They seemed to understand, but NY didn't take it so well, so she had to put her foot down with him and let him know that her mental health was much more important than his imagined need for her; besides, she knew that he had a girlfriend.

So, Charlie would go without sex, while trying to figure out what she wanted to do. But while she was going through this period, she had reaffirmed that sex was definitely a need for her. Her decision to leave all her lovers alone wasn't a good one. She fell into a depression, then realized that sex had always been an antidepressant for her. That endorphin boost that came from sex was important to her mental health. She knew that the lack of sex wasn't *causing* the depression, but not having sex was prolonging it. She might have to make a phone call and rescind her self-imposed sexual hiatus.

Some of the things that she came to understand better, was the importance of each of her friends to her life. Lowell was a big sweet teddy bear, who she liked talking to, and she loved his hugs and kisses. He just made her feel loved, with his affectionate touches, and long aggressive kisses. New York was a young man full of life and energy, and full of lust. This made sex with him fun, exciting, and nasty. She loved his fetishes and enjoyed giving in to them. She respected his understanding of what he liked sexually, something that not all men could communicate, and that's if they even knew what they really liked. He communicated his desires well, which helped Charlie to give him everything that he wanted. She would get turned on by knowing that she was turning her partner on, so the more she understood about his desires, the more she could please him, and the deeper her orgasms.

Something else that she had to come to terms with, was her feelings for Zhon. Before she ended their sexual relationship, she had to really think long and hard. Her feelings for him went really deep, but she always kept them under control. Partially because he never seemed to have any deep feelings for her, beyond their friendship; also, because she knew at some point he would meet someone that he would marry. She rationalized her feelings into suppression.

By doing that, she was realizing that she was hurting her own emotional growth. Even though she swore not to ever fall in love with a man, before he fell for her, during her time of rebuilding her self-esteem, time had softened her; and the wall around her heart was crumbling. And much of that was due to Zhon, and how he helped her to learn to trust again, and how he accepted her for who she was, and how he continued to respect her, no matter what crazy things she revealed to him about herself. In her eyes, he possessed all the qualities that she would ever want in a man if she ever got into a committed relationship.

It was as if she were being punished for something that she did, to finally meet someone who she would give her all for, but because she had exposed so much of herself to him in honesty and friendship, (in her mind) these would be the same things that would keep her from being able to be with him; and that's if he would've even wanted that, and she never felt like he did.

I Made a Mistake.

One day, during Charlies time of temporary, self-imposed abstinence, she and Zhon had some playful back and forth texting, when Zhon offered to help put an end to her sexual drought. He was playing and had no idea that Charlie needed that to happen, like yesterday. So, Charlie told him to bring it on. Their sexual relationship was far more involved than any she ever had, because not only was it physical, it was also mental for her, and it ran the gamut of cyber-sex too.

So, Zhon thought that she was playing, but wasn't sure at this point. He commented that she was confusing him because he thought that she had ended their sexual relationship. Charlie agreed that she did end it, but she needed some sex, and if he wanted to be the one who gave it to her, that she would welcome it. Zhon just laughed it off, and Charlie realized that she was coming across as wishy-washy, and it was important for her to explain things to Zhon to prevent that incorrect assessment of her. So, she sent him an email explaining everything that was going on with her.

Zhon received her email and wasn't really sure what to make of it, so he called her.

"What's going on Charlie? Talk to me!"

"I'm just going through some emotional confusion, and I thought that ending our sexual relationship was somehow going to help. I've become afraid of my emotional state while living my lifestyle; the two can't co-exist. So, I haven't been having sex with anyone, but I've also fallen into a depression. And what I'm realizing is that the sex has always kept depression at bay for me; it's been my antidepressant. So now, not only am I depressed, I'm not giving myself what I need to help combat my depression. That's why I changed my mind about us having sex.

I've also realized how deep my feelings are for you. This is so hard for me to say, but not saying it is eating me up. I love you, and no matter how hard I try to fight it or deny it, I cannot shake you from my heart. And it doesn't matter how you feel about me because this is about what you mean to me and my life. We are two different individuals with different needs from the opposite sex, and you happen to fill most of mine by being who you are to me.

Your friendship is invaluable. You've been my shoulder to lean on, albeit usually cyberly, and my confidant, and I've been able to tell you things about my thoughts and myself that I have never told anyone. And that's because I feel a trust in you that I've never had before, along with feeling like you really understand me. And my attraction to you is, Sheesh!!! I just think you're the sexiest, most handsome, most intelligent man I've ever known. And the *sex*…, the sex takes me to a place that I never knew existed, and I'm someone who has always loved and enjoyed sex. Your aggression and your sexual ways just do something to me. They match my needs on a primal level. And the cyber-sex that we have, is just crazy fun and exciting.

I know that this is a lot that I'm telling you, and I hope that it doesn't make you too uncomfortable, but I needed to say these things. But I also understand if these revelations cause you to fall back, and I wouldn't blame you one bit if you did."

Charlie would end her conversation there, nervous about how Zhon would respond, but his response was to tell her that she needed to do whatever was necessary to get back to her happiness. This left Charlie a little empty, but she understood. She also felt relieved to finally get her feelings for him off her chest. It would help her to move on, without any regrets. She no longer would have to fight with herself to tell him the truth about how she felt since she always put up a strong front as someone who didn't need an emotional connection to any man, and as someone who wasn't interested in being in love or in a relationship. She understood that she did this to herself and had to accept accountability for it, and she would. She knew that she would hurt for a while but would do all that was necessary to get through it.

Charlie wouldn't hear from Zhon for weeks. She would never regret the choice, to be honest with anyone, so her reaction to his apparent distancing himself from her, was for her to leave him be. All things must come to an end, at some point, and she felt that this was their end.

The Surprise.

Charlie was restocking the café with liquor, coffee, and teas. She had already restocked the crackers and cheeses the week before, and the cakes, pies, and other desserts were a daily delivery. Devon was waiting on guests when she saw Zhon come in, so she was unable to greet him without shouting across the café. He walked to the back of the café where Charlie was, and she had her back to the counter when he asked for some coffee. The voice was familiar, but she had to turn around to identify it. When she saw that it was Zhon, her face lit up like a Christmas tree. The last person she expected to see, but the only one who could make her face and heart light up like he did.

"What are you doing here?" Charlie said with a surprised, but happy voice.

"I came to see you!"

"No, I meant what are you doing in town. I know that you didn't come here for the coffee."

She laughed, then walked around the counter to give him a long, hard, hug. She didn't really care why he was in town, she just didn't know what else to say at that moment.

"How have you been?" Charlie asked.

"I'm great! Miss talking to you, but great!"

"Yeah, yeah, yeah, whatever!" she said playfully and laughed.

"I was hoping to scratch your itch if you still need a tune-up."

She cracked up laughing. "Am I an itchy bitch, or a car, *jeesh*!!" She laughed again.

Zhon laughed, "Neither, I just want to feel that warm, wet pussy wrapped around my dick!"

Charlie went right into horny mode, with his dirty talk. She couldn't wait to have sex with him again. She let Devon run the café so that she and Zhon could meet up at her condo. They would have sex several times that day, and Charlie couldn't pull herself together to go back to the café. After Zhon left, she felt like she was drugged. The sex with him put her in a state of euphoric bliss for the rest of the day. She needed that *badly*!!! And she needed him even *more*!!! This would hopefully start the decline of her depression. It didn't end it, but with other things that she would do, over the next few weeks, her depression subsided.

Zhon had to go back home, but Charlie restarted her sexual relationships with Lowell and New York again. She couldn't care less about getting into a committed relationship at this point. She could never be that chick who waits until she's in a relationship to have sex. She thanked God that she lived during a time of female liberation, or she would have been stigmatized or repressed, in a past life.

Living and Loving Life

Charlie came to terms with the fact that she loved her life with her three lovers. As many times that she attempted to end each relationship for different reasons, she could never meet anyone to fill the void of those relationships. Even having two out of three lovers couldn't fill the void of the third. They each affected her in their own unique ways. She even tried allowing herself to meet other men and even went out with them, but she usually couldn't get to a place where she wanted to be intimate with them; she just wasn't feeling it. And when she did feel it, the guys who she was attracted to had deep-rooted issues that Charlie couldn't accept.

Charlie had read an article on "The Dialogical Self", and it explained how we all have multiple personalities within us. How we act differently in different environments and around different people. Most of us can understand this when we talk about how we act around our friends, versus how we act at work. These are two different parts of who we are, and we understand the need to be these different individuals. It's the same when you are one way around your family, and a different way around your mate, or lover. These are once again two more of our personalities.

This made sense to Charlie, to the point that she knew that she didn't want to give up any of her lovers. They each fulfilled needs within her, even outside of the sex. She also felt like this, in some small way, helped her to understand the need for some people to cheat. One of those personalities within us needs to come out and play. Although this seems like a cop out, she still felt like this need may be a small factor in infidelity. It also explained in her mind how some men could have entire second families without either family knowing about each other.

There are some men who get to do this without the betrayal of infidelity and mendacity. Think 'Big Love', or some within other faiths where men are allowed more than one wife.

Perhaps the reason why women don't do it is because of the patriarchal society that we live in (although Charlie understood that it was coming to an end), and the fact that women would be labeled for having the same thoughts, desires, and behaviors as men. Perhaps because things were shifting away from patriarchy, women like her can allow themselves to enjoy more than one man, and to allow the different personalities inside themselves to express themselves.

Charlie always understood the power of three, and that always worked for her in many areas of her life. Three men were the perfect number for her. That would be her limit of comfort. Three satisfied enough of her personalities to provide contentment. There was no betrayal because there was no commitment, and there were also no lies or the need for any, from her end in any of these relationships.

For now, Charlie had what she needed in male companionship. And she was also able to maintain the freedom that she greatly desired and appreciated. She also appreciated the men in her life for their respect of her and her need for her freedom. An understanding that she couldn't just get from anyone. This and many other reasons made these men special to her life, and she tried to express her gratitude to each of them.

Once she mentally stripped the instilled societal messages and traditions from her life's structure, she understood her own wants and needs in life. Charlie was very much content with her life, just as it was. She loved her singleness, and the freedom of having her own, including her own bedroom and bed that she didn't have to share with anyone. Her bedroom was set up specifically for her and all her idiosyncrasies. She knew that if she had a partner, she would have to compromise the perfection of her bedroom as it was for her, to accommodate a partner; she would have to share her space every night. It would no longer be her perfect solace from the world because she would have someone else's energy to contend with. She would no longer have her peace and quiet, something that she greatly appreciated as an accomplishment from the constant drama of her early years.

She wondered if she could even go back to being with one man. It's almost like opening Pandora's Box. Once you open it, you cannot close it and undo all those things that were experienced and relegated into the deep recesses of the mind. Once those experiences are known, they are known forever. Will the mundaneness that happens in relationships, cause a desire for the excitement of her former life? Would it be fair to her partner if she were to end the relationship out of boredom? Would that show a lack of strength and perseverance? She knew that she lacked neither, and would be greatly insulted by such an evaluation.

The thought of it all seemed so stressful and unnecessary. Remaining single would always seem the perfect relationship status for her. She could have her freedom, and enjoy her special friends when the time was right for them. The sporadic visits that would happen, fit right into her aversion to routine and monotony. This also prevented the complacency that happens in so many relationships, that lead into the boredom that she so greatly disliked. Boredom for her could lead to depression, a state of mind that she tried to avoid at all cost.

Charlie suffered a depression in her early adulthood and marriage, that made her question life itself. It was a severe depression that took her to a place where she understood the motivation for suicide. A depression where she fought for her life, mentally and physically, and won. A depression that she never wanted to experience again in life. This was a major reason that she fought to always do things that would make her happy, and make her feel alive. She was grateful for her life, and although many of her experiences were emotionally painful, and some were frightening, learning to overcome those things gave her strength.

Is it Love?

Zhon never told Charlie that he loved her, and he may not even believe that what he feels for her is love, but everything about his actions and lack thereof, said a love of some kind; she understood this. Society and its rules had a way of ruining love, because of all the expectations that are put on the idea of love. So, proof of love comes from many material things that have nothing to do with real love.

The social pressures of having money spent buying things, and giving and getting gifts, holiday gifts, birthday gifts, anniversary gifts, gifts of all kind; and all the monetary expectations is somehow a proof of love. And even if a person understands that it isn't, their friends and family will have plenty to say about it. Keeping the relationship clandestine takes all that pressure away from both parties.

Her un-comfortability with accepting money and gifts from men made this a non-issue for Charlie. Her ex-husband's decision to use money in an attempt to control her, caused her to see it in that light with all men, as a means to control women. Even though she knew that all men weren't that way, her experience, and the stories that she would hear from other women, and see from other men, would cause Charlie to have issues with accepting any type of financial help and gifts from the men she would come in contact with. When a woman accepts money and gifts from a man, this can leave them feeling indebted to them, and Charlie wanted no parts of that feeling; she would owe no man, anything.

A social revelation of their relationship would strongly change the dynamics of it, because of societies expectations of what a relationship should be. Also, other people will always try to define love for someone else, but no one could define Charlie's experience of love for her.

She knew what she felt was love for Zhon, and she also felt what she got from him was love. We often use the phrase "Actions speak louder than words", and if we believe in that phrase, then Zhon's actions denoted love, to Charlie. Does a person always have to say the words "I love you", to express love? It's nice to hear, but how many say it without meaning it. Charlie's father never told her that he loved her, yet she never questioned her father's love for her, for she felt it every-day in his deeds, his tone, and his protection of her.

Zhon may not even view his feelings as love, based on what he believes love is. His understanding of her, his acceptance of her, his unwavering friendship, their sexual connection, the fact that those connections remain no matter how many lovers they each go through, gave Charlie the feeling that a transcendence of love had become the foundation of their friendship.

Although Charlie understood that a sexual connection didn't really have a lot to do with real love (no one understood that more than Charlie), she didn't believe that the intensity of the connection with Zhon could exist without it. She had many lovers in the past, even a couple who she cared for deeply, but the connection was nothing like it was with Zhon. Even their physical distance couldn't break any of their bonds, even when she expected it to.

Even if Zhon didn't love her, her love for him had nothing to do with how he felt about her. It was not defined by societies rules of what love is supposed to be, and she didn't come to the conclusion of love easily. She took herself through a lot of turmoil trying to tell herself that she wasn't in love with him, but when she stopped trying to define love as something two people had to feel together, she was able to accept what she was feeling as love; whether he felt it or not, didn't matter anymore.

When you understand the history of love and think about the great love stories of Tristan and Isolde, or Guinevere and Lancelot, and many untold love stories between common men and women of royalty or affluence, you start to see that love between two people has no prerequisite. Many time's these love affairs were never consummated or able to play themselves out, because they were forced to end for many valid social reasons of the times.

Perhaps the struggle to physically engage in, or consummate these love affairs, helps to keep them sacred and forever, for if they were able to play themselves out, maybe they would end the way that many committed relationships of modern times end; in betrayal and hate. Some with the amicable understanding that it's best to part ways.

The distance of Zhon and Charlie may be the very thing that will safeguard her love for him, forever. The longing that Charlie may have felt from time to time has subsided in time. Their sexy phone calls, and his sporadic visits a few times a year, made the sex all the more special. And if you think about how couples can't keep their hands off each other in the beginning of their relationships, and how after time passes, the passion defuses, and sex is less often, you can see how time and distance can help to preserve that passion.

Another thought that has entered Charlie's mind, is the fact that she is a free-spirit. Could she even handle being in a committed relationship with someone who she knew believed in a certain structure for relationships, namely, marriage? Someone who had a lot of social commitments like church, fraternities, and social groups. She couldn't see herself being a dutiful partner, in these areas. She also didn't like being a part of groups, because she had a hard time conforming to anything and joining something that she couldn't strictly follow, which was most things. She couldn't stand to be told how she had to act to prove support for anything. She would support what she wanted, however, she chose to do that.

Charlie realized that her thoughts were her mind rationalizing the situation, in order to cope with her feelings for Zhon. This had become a natural skill for her, to remain mentally strong. Would she be with him if the chance ever presented itself? She absolutely would. She understood that the experience was more important than the end result of that experience, in order to live the fullest life, without regret.

You should never run from the opportunity for happiness. All happy times have eventual interference. You should enjoy them for their duration and appreciate the gift that it is. What kind of life would it be if happy was our constant state of mind? All states of mind can become adaptive when prolonged, but life always interferes with that state. In order to appreciate happiness, you have to live in the world and fall into other states of mind and emotions, and Charlie understood this.

Lisa A. Forrest is an emerging book writer with many stories to tell. She lives on the outskirts of her hometown of Philadelphia, PA, in Boothwyn, PA.

You can follow her blogs at:
www.therealfountainofyouth.family
&
Her Parlons Café Facebook page at:
https://www.facebook.com/lisaaforrest2018/

90307144R00098

Made in the USA
Columbia, SC
01 March 2018